A Love to Treasure

Sunriver Dreams Series

A Love to Treasure

A Love to Treasure

SUNRIVER DREAMS BOOK ONE

By
Kimberly Rose Johnson

A Love to Treasure

A Love to Treasure
Published by Mountain Brook Ink
White Salmon, WA U.S.A.

The website addresses recommended throughout this book are offered as a resource. These websites are not intended in any way to be or imply an endorsement on the part of Mountain Brook Ink, nor do we vouch for their content.

This story is a work of fiction. All characters and events are the product of the author's imagination. Any resemblance to any person, living or dead, is coincidental.

Scripture quotations are taken from the King James Version of the Bible. Public domain.
ISBN 978-1-943959-08-2
© 2016 Kimberly R. Johnson

The Team: Miralee Ferrell, Kathryn Davis, Nikki Wright, Cindy Jackson
Cover Design: Indie Cover Design, Lynnette Bonner Designer

Mountain Brook Ink is an inspirational publisher offering fiction you can believe in.

Printed in the United States of America

ACKNOWLEDGMENTS

I would like to thank everyone who had a hand it making this book happen, from the proofreaders to my publisher and everyone in between. Without the critiques from multiple critique partners, you know who you are, my editor, publisher, and proofreaders, this book would not be what it is.

Thank you, everyone!

CHAPTER ONE

NICOLE DAVIS DROVE PAST A HUGE welcome sign to Sunriver, Oregon, and grinned. She was finally here. She loved this resort community and still couldn't believe it would be her home for the next few months.

She bore to the right around the traffic circle. Suddenly a black car came out of nowhere. Nicole swerved and slammed on the brake, her front bumper barely missing the side of the black car. Her heart pounded as she weaved her Mini Cooper S onto the miniscule dirt shoulder a few feet from a large pine tree. She put the car in park, her breath coming in quick puffs. She looked around to make sure she hadn't hit anything. *Whew.* Everything looked okay.

The crazy driver who ran her off the road drove around the circle again and pulled off the road in front of her. This couldn't be good. She gulped as a dark-haired man wearing jeans and a dark gray T-shirt stalked toward her.

Her gut clenched. She checked her reflection in the rearview mirror and noted her wide green eyes filled with fear. *Not good.* She needed to appear unaffected by the incident or he'd see her vulnerability. She took a deep breath then let it out in a whoosh. After making sure no cars were coming, she stepped out of her Mini Cooper and onto the shoulder, refusing to be intimidated by the man. His height caught her by surprise. Most men were only a few inches taller than she was, but not this guy. He towered above her five-foot-nine-inch frame. And those biceps—maybe she should've stayed in the car. But he didn't look dangerous, only irritated.

She offered him a tentative smile. "That was a close call."

"No kidding. You didn't yield." He pointed to a yellow sign.

"Oops. Sorry." Her face heated. Grams always said she barreled through life. However, she generally obeyed traffic signs. "I didn't see the sign."

She focused on the handsome man before her with close-cropped hair and dark brown eyes the color of Swiss chocolate.

His brows turned down. "Are you okay?"

Her gaze dropped to his mouth, which was pulled into a frown. She shook her head and focused on the concern in his eyes. "I'm fine. No harm done, as they say. And I really am sorry about not yielding." She backed against the car door. Her grandmother had paid for this adventure, and she *would* enjoy it—she just needed to be more careful. "I haven't been to Sunriver in years and was trying to find the resort lodge." She took in her surroundings—a paved bicycle trail, roadway, and woods. Beyond the woods, she spotted several structures dotting the landscape. "I don't suppose you could point me in the right direction."

He peered down at her, his stance relaxing. He even ventured what appeared to be a small smile. "Like you said, no harm done." He pointed slightly left. "The lodge is that way."

The breeze rustling through the tall pine trees didn't help the heat burning in Nicole's cheeks. "Thanks."

"No problem. Watch for the signs. They'll keep you on track." He sauntered back to his car, then pivoted. "By the way, welcome to Sunriver. I hope the rest of your stay goes better."

"Uh, thanks." Nicole slid behind the wheel and drove away, hoping she wouldn't run into that man again. Talk about embarrassing! She breathed in deeply of the pine-scented air and focused on her reason for being here—Grams' letter. She owed it to her grandmother to fulfill her final wish.

Nicole turned left into the lodge's parking lot and pulled into a spot. The lodge was even prettier than she remembered. The planters, a combination of red, purple and white flowers mixed among shrubs and trees, were perfection. She got out, grabbed her luggage, and walked toward the grand entrance. A young couple strolled hand-in-hand nearby, and several people dressed in business attire ambled out of the lodge. The sound of crashing water drew her attention. A beautiful rock water feature off to the right of the main entrance looked like the perfect place to escape the busyness of life.

She dragged her attention away from the waterfall and climbed the concrete steps to the entrance. The huge door opened with surprising ease. She pulled off her sunglasses and allowed her eyes to adjust to the dim lighting. Straight ahead, stairs led to a restaurant where a few guests milled about. To her left, several smartly dressed people stood behind a counter waiting to check in guests.

Nicole squared her shoulders and marched toward check-in trying to ignore the knot in the pit of her stomach. Why was she so nervous? Grams had loved scavenger hunts, and this vacation promised to be an adventure, beginning with the letter that led her to the resort.

Nicole approached the first person at the long reception counter. "Hi, I'm Nicole Davis. I have a reservation."

The woman smiled. "Welcome to Sunriver. I love your hair color. Is it natural?"

Nicole nodded. "Yes and thanks." Grams had loved her long blonde hair as well.

"You're lucky." She lowered her voice. "Mine's from a bottle." She sighed then clicked on the computer keyboard. She raised a brow. "You have a package. I'll be right back."

A package—*so the game begins*. Grams had a creative streak few could compete with. The package would likely contain the first clue to this adventure Grams had sent her on.

The woman came back and held out a small box wrapped in

bright red paper with a shiny white bow on top.

"Thank you."

"You're welcome." She handed her a key card, then showed her where her room was on the map and explained how to get to it. "Enjoy your stay."

Nicole pocketed the key. "Thanks. I'll try." She left the building and followed the path to the stairwell that led to her nearby suite. What was in the box? Whatever it was, she knew Grams had put a lot of thought into it.

Nicole's throat burned at the thought of her late Grandmother—so much regret. If only she'd spent more time with Grams and less time working on lesson plans this past year. She'd loved her grandmother and wished for a do-over, but death didn't have do-overs. Instead, Nicole would honor her grandmother's final wish and play along one last time. Hopefully this game wouldn't end in disaster like the time she'd ended up in the middle of a lake with a broken oar.

AFTER CHANGING INTO HIS uniform, Mark Stone strapped on a helmet and straddled his bicycle outside the Sunriver police department. Soon heat would rise from the pavement and make him long for the cooler paths winding through the tall pine trees. Hopefully his first day on the job would go better than the drive getting here. If all the tourists were like that blonde . . . oh, boy. But he had to give her credit for admitting her mistake. She seemed like a nice enough person, and she was definitely easy to look at with her long hair and emerald green eyes.

"Morning." A stocky officer strode up with his hand extended. "I'm Spencer. If you need anything, let me know."

"Mark Stone. Thanks." He grasped the younger man's hand and gave it a firm shake. Spencer looked to be in his late twenties, with sandy blond hair and piercing eyes. He reminded Mark of himself at that age—eager and ready to take on the world, but that was then. Life had a way of changing a person.

Spencer's eyebrows narrowed. "I heard you like working alone."

Mark gave him an easy grin. Seemed the rumor mill worked overtime if they were talking about him. "True." An image exploded in his mind, knocking him back to another time and place—the reason he no longer worked with a partner. The reason he'd fled Portland, Oregon, and come to the resort town. Thankfully, his superiors were more than happy to let him work alone due to budget issues.

"Guess I'd better get busy. Nice to meet you."

Spencer nodded, then headed inside. He seemed like someone Mark wouldn't mind getting to know despite his digging into a sore subject. Mark shook off the thought and pushed forward, focusing on the paved trail in front of him.

He passed a couple jogging and settled into an easy rhythm. One thing was certain; he'd be in great shape by summer's end. Cool air brushed his face. In a fenced pasture, tall grass swayed in the breeze. He could definitely get used to this. Sunriver was a far cry from the intensity of working in the big city.

He braked at a stop sign before crossing the road and went left along the path that ran past the stables. The only sound was the whir of his tires on the pavement. He caught up to three bicycle riders in no particular hurry. "On your left."

The women moved their bikes into single file. The middle woman looked over her shoulder, wobbled, and a mere second later bumped into the leader. She yelped, and the two went down. The last bike couldn't avoid the heap and joined the jumbled bodies.

Mark braked hard and jumped off. Bending over the women, he peered down and scanned for injuries. "Anyone hurt?"

Silence greeted his question. His heart hammered. He

assessed each of the women quickly but couldn't see any visible injuries.

The women met each other's eyes. Then a soft snort escaped the redhead. The woman to her right erupted in a fit of giggles. In a moment, the three of them were leaning against each other, laughing.

He squatted to their level. "I take it everyone is okay." He grinned and offered his hand.

"Yes, officer." The redhead brushed her palms together, then grasped his hand. "I guess I shouldn't have followed so closely."

He pulled her up before offering a hand to her friend.

A dark haired woman rolled her eyes. "Tina, you and tailgating go together like peanut butter and jelly. Come on. Let's get a move on before Connor gets too far ahead of us."

"Connor?" Mark couldn't squelch his curiosity.

The woman nodded and brushed her hands against her denim shorts. "Yes, my twelve-year-old cousin is visiting for the summer, and believe me, he's a handful." She pursed her lips. "Maybe I shouldn't have said that. I simply meant—"

"Don't worry, I understand." Mark chuckled. "I was a handful myself at his age."

The woman gave him a grateful smile. "I'm Sarah and these are my reckless friends, Tina and Marge."

Tina righted her bike and blatantly checked out Mark. "We're staying in Sarah's Circle Four Ranch Cabin. Would you like to join us tonight for a barbecue? It's the least we can do, considering."

The other two nodded.

"Sorry, ladies, but thanks for the offer."

Tina slipped a business card into his hand and winked. "Call me."

The women mounted their bikes and pedaled away.

Mark rubbed his neck. That was awkward, but at least they were gone, and he'd dodged their dinner invitation. Nothing against assertive women, but that trio left him feeling like a piece of meat. He much preferred the blonde who ran him off the road—not that it mattered.

He couldn't get the defiant look in her eyes out of his mind, and it made him want to get to know her. The thought sent him reeling.

CHAPTER TWO

SHADE COVERED A SMALL PORTION OF the green lawn that surrounded the sparkling water in the North Pool in Sunriver. Nicole wore a perfect fitting, black, one-piece swimsuit she'd found in the package. How had Grams known? The attached clue had been odd. She could still see it in her mind's eye.

The North Pool was a favorite of mine. Take a dip and see what you find when the long arm touches six and the short arm one. The color of the day is RED. What did red mean? Was there something red in the bottom of the pool? She stood and walked to the edge of the pool and peered into the clear water. Nothing. She returned to her seat. The rest of the clue had to mean whatever would happen would take place at one-thirty. It was one-twenty-five now.

The lifeguards wore red, but what would a lifeguard have to do with Grams' game? She sat on the edge of a white lounge chair and tapped her toe. Bodies of all shapes and sizes splashed in the pool several feet away from her. She fanned her face with her hand.

A young boy jumped into the water and droplets sprayed across her legs, shockingly refreshing. Maybe a quick dip in the pool would feel good. She looked at the inviting water, wishing for the cool relief from the heat. If she understood the clue correctly, she still had a few minutes. But if she missed whatever it was Grams had planned . . . she sighed and leaned back in the chair. Better wait.

Children squealed in delight as they played in the water nearby. Grams would have gotten a kick out of watching the kids play. Why did she have to die? How did a person move past the pain? A month since the funeral, and she didn't feel any closer to healing. Maybe that was what this game was all about—moving on. But she didn't want to move on. She loved Grams and would forever hold her memory close.

A raucous laugh grabbed her attention. She tilted her head to see what was so funny. Three women were having the time of their lives over something and behaving as if they were the only ones at the pool.

"I can't believe you gave him your number, Tina." A brunette gave her friend a playful shove. "Did you forget you have a boyfriend?"

"That tall drink of water had the brownest eyes I've ever seen. Totally mesmerizing. I couldn't help myself."

"Mesmerizing? You're so dramatic!" Her friend tossed a flip-flop at the one named Tina.

Tina sighed. "Honey, it comes with the trade." Tina sighed. "Now I'd take *him* as my leading man any day. Mmm-hmm."

The third woman harrumphed. "Give me a break. Sure, he was perfect, but you *both* have boyfriends. And I don't think acting in community theater counts."

"Of course it does," Tina purred. "I may have another job that pays the bills, but I'm an actress to the core. And as far as having a boyfriend goes, that doesn't keep us from looking."

"You told him to call you, Tina!"

Tina laughed. "I'm on vacation. Besides he turned me down flat, so it's a moot point."

Nicole couldn't stop the grin that stretched her lips when she thought about the man they described. He sounded easy on the eyes. But no one was *that* perfect.

She listened to the women tease one another a moment longer, then leaned back and closed her eyes. She used to have close friends, but had lost touch with them. Life had gotten in the way. Maybe her old boyfriend had been right when he accused her of putting work and school before everyone. An ache of loneliness settled over her, and she wished for a do-over in the social department, too. But that wasn't likely. Most of her friends were married and starting families. Not her. Grams had been her family until cancer cut her life short.

"Cannonball!" A huge splash of water sprayed onto the pool deck. Nicole jumped as the cold water hit her skin. Her eyes flew open, and she spotted a boy probably around twelve or thirteen with a wide grin and a mischievous look in his eyes.

"Connor Gray Davidson!" One of the women who'd been talking earlier stood and propped her hands on her waist. "That was rude."

The boy shrugged and plastered on an innocent face. "Sorry. I was only having fun."

"Well, stop." She spun around and caught Nicole gaping at the scene. "Sorry about my cousin. He forgets he's not the only one here."

"It's fine. I needed to be cooled off anyway. It was just . . . a shock."

"Ha. I'll say. He's visiting me for the summer, and every day seems to be a new shock." She frowned. "Who knew boys could be such a handful?"

Nicole laughed. "He's not *that* bad. You can't expect me to believe you never did a cannonball as a girl." She sent the boy a conspiratorial wink as he rested his elbows on the side of the pool and listened in. "Cannonballs are way too much fun for to resist."

"I suppose you're right." A lopsided grin lit Sarah's face. "Thanks for understanding. Hey, you're getting quite a burn." She pointed to Nicole's shoulder.

Nicole turned her head and spotted bright red skin. "Oh no!" She reached in her bag for a cover up that cascaded to her elbows. "Thanks. I'm Nicole."

"Nice to meet you. I'm Sarah and these are my friends, Tina and Marge." The women waved. Sarah moved toward the pool.

"You coming in, Nicole?"

"Sure." She could keep the cover-up on in the water and whoever or whatever she waited poolside for could wait for *her*—one-thirty had come and passed. For the first time since Grams' death she didn't feel lonely, and she liked that feeling. Nicole stood and stopped short when an older guy waved her over. Her pulse kicked up a notch—he wore red.

"Are you Nicole Davis?"

"Yes. But how'd you know?"

He waved a snapshot of her from her last birthday.

She caught her breath. "Where'd you get that?"

"It was taped to the outside." He held up a manila envelope and handed it to her. "I'm sorry I'm late. I got the message to deliver this a few minutes ago but couldn't get away sooner."

"No problem. Thanks. Who sent you?" This must be the next clue. Good thing he got here, or she'd have turned into a crispy lobster waiting for him. She knew better than to come to the pool without sunblock, especially with her fair skin, but Grams' game had her brain muddled.

He smiled and raised a brow. "I can't say. I've never been asked to deliver something like this before. It feels so cloak and dagger—like something out of *Mission Impossible*."

She laughed and raised the envelope. "Thanks." Maybe an old movie had inspired Grams, but she doubted it.

Sarah and her friends were in the pool and didn't seem to notice she'd been sidetracked. Should she take a dip or open the clue? She looked toward the pool again. The promise of cooling off in the water and forging a friendship tempted her, but she was here for one reason, and now she had what she'd come for. It was time to see what the big mystery was.

Nicole sat and tore open the envelope, then drew out a single sheet of paper with a key taped to it.

"Sunshine poolside is always a good idea. Relaxation at its finest. This key is the beginning of your adventure. Don't forget to keep your

eyes open and enjoy the world around you. Have fun, sweetie. Love always, Grams."

Nicole held up the key and sighed. "What am I supposed to do with this?" Water dripped near her feet, and she looked up. "Oh, hi, Sarah. Sorry I never made it to the pool." She held up the envelope and key. "I got sidetracked."

Sarah wrapped herself in an oversized towel and plopped down beside her. "What's the key for?"

"My grandma was big on adventures. Before she died. she wrote me a letter I was supposed to open upon her death. In it, she asked me to go to Sunriver as soon as school released for the summer. So here I am."

"I'm sorry about your grandma."

"Thanks. She was quite a lady. Always putting others before herself. Case in point, this game she left for me. I know she'll never know if I played along or not, but I want to do it for her because it would have made her happy." Sadness gripped Nicole, threatening to pull her into a pool of grief, but she shook it off and plastered on a smile. "Anyway, she left me clues to follow."

"Sounds like fun. You mentioned school. Are you a college student?"

Nicole shook her head. "Teacher." She frowned. "At least I was. The school where I worked had to make cutbacks, and since this was my first year, they didn't renew my contract."

"Ouch."

"Tell me about it." She'd applied at a few schools around Oregon, but none of those jobs really appealed. What she really wanted was her old job back, or better yet, a job here in Sunriver. Now that would be incredible. She'd have to check the district website and see if they were hiring. If they were, she'd be sure to apply. It would be a dream come true to live and work here.

Sarah stared at Nicole's shoulders. "You really need to put ointment on your shoulders. I can see the red through your cover-up."

"That doesn't sound good. Maybe I should go."

"Wait. I have a fix for your burn. Be right back." Sarah grabbed something from her bag and came back. "This stuff will help." She held up a spray can. "It has aloe in it and feels soothing on a burn. You can buy your own at the grocery store in the village, but this should help until then."

"Thanks." Nicole removed her cover-up and held her breath as Sarah sprayed her shoulders. "Brr. It's freezing."

"Doesn't it feel nice though?"

"Mmm. Yes." The cold sank through the burning hot layers of skin bringing sweet relief. She chuckled. "To think a few minutes ago I was roasting."

"Glad I could help." Sarah snapped the cap back on the can.

"I'll be sure to get that stuff. Thanks for the tip."

"You're welcome." Sarah looked toward her friends, then back at Nicole. "I grab coffee at the Merchant Trader Café every morning. Would you like to join me tomorrow?"

Nicole tipped her head to the side. "I'd love to. Your friends won't mind?"

"Nope. I jog in the mornings and then stop for coffee and a bagel at the café before walking back to my cabin. I'd love company."

"You're sure your friends won't change their mind?"

"Trust me, they don't get up before eleven, and my cousin sleeps late too. They're all on vacation. I, on the other hand, am not. I took the day off to spend with them, but it's back to work for me tomorrow. I'll be at the café in the lodge by seven. Is that too early for you?"

"Not at all. I'm a morning person."

"Good. I'll see you then." Sarah turned and rejoined her friends, who had sauntered back to sun themselves on the lounge chairs.

Nicole had had more than enough heat and gathered her stuff. She needed to figure out what this key went to.

CHAPTER THREE

MARK EASED INTO THE HAMMOCK WITH a groan and closed his eyes. He draped his arm over the side and ran his hand along Sadie's back. He'd recently adopted the Golden Retriever and didn't have one regret. Talk about a good dog.

He shifted and stifled a groan. Every muscle in his body ached. No one warned him to take it easy his first day, but they sure had a good laugh at his expense when he could barely walk after getting off the bike.

Sadie sat up and growled.

"What is it, girl?" Footsteps on the deck had Mark twisting to see who was approaching. The hammock tilted to one side and dumped him to the ground as Sadie darted out of the way.

She barked at Spencer, one of his new co-workers.

"It's okay, girl." Mark scrambled to standing, and every muscle in his backside screamed at him. The blasted hammock needed adjusting so that wouldn't happen again.

Sadie quieted and sat, never taking her gaze off the other officer.

Spencer chuckled as he folded his six-foot frame into one of the plastic Adirondack chairs. "Nice dog."

"Thanks. What brings you by?"

"Wanted to see how your day went. I had your job my rookie year, and that first week was murder."

Mark winced at Spencer's choice of words, as he eased into the other Adirondack chair. Murder—he shook off the all too fresh memory, and focused on the man across from him. "Today was quiet. You have any action?"

"I responded to a burglary and a fender bender."

"A burglary?" His gut tightened. Sunriver was supposed to be quiet.

"Yeah. There've been a string of them this past week."

Mark frowned. It seemed crime wove its tentacles everywhere. "Any leads?"

"Only that all the houses hit are part of the same rental pool."

"Inside job?"

Spencer shrugged. "Could be. There's nothing pointing to that, but we're still investigating."

"Let me know if I can help." Mark almost revealed he'd been a detective in Portland, but stopped himself in time. That would create too many questions since he was working well beneath his rank and abilities this summer.

"Thanks, but I don't think a rookie will be much help. No offense."

Mark's pulse quickened at the jab—he had at least five years of experience on the man. He shook off the comment. The chief agreed to keep his experience quiet, but the slight rankled just the same. "No offense taken, but the offer stands if you need a fresh perspective."

Spencer nodded and stood. "You work tomorrow?"

"Yes." Hopefully he'd be able to straddle the seat.

"See you then." Spencer hopped off the deck and sauntered across the dirt to the driveway.

Mark frowned. He'd wanted a light workload with limited threat potential, but if his investigative skills were needed maybe he should offer his services to the chief. Then again, he'd been ordered by his boss to relax this summer. That might prove to be easier said than done if someone was burglarizing rental units. He'd need to be extra vigilant to look for suspicious behavior while he was patrolling.

Frightened screams from the direction of the bike trail

behind his rental had him leaping to his feet despite his protesting muscles. Adrenaline pumping, he jumped off the deck. Sadie scrambled after him then ran beside him as he sprinted across the dirt, littered with grasses and lava rocks. He headed toward the trail keeping watch for threats as he charged across the dry landscape. Water balloon remains littered the bike path. He looked around but didn't spot anyone. A balloon splashed at his feet, then another exploded against his gut. He sprinted in the direction the balloon had come.

A boy ran from behind a boulder. He looked to be about five feet tall, with brown hair a little too long to be considered clean cut. He wore jeans and a gray T-shirt.

"Sadie, stay!" Mark sprinted, then reached out and grabbed the back of the kid's shirt. "Hold up."

"Let me go! I didn't hurt anyone." The kid thrashed, trying to pull away.

He gripped the boy's shoulder. "Cool it! I'm not going to hurt you. I only want to talk."

The boy stilled. "What do you want?" He eyed Mark with distrust.

"What's your name?"

"Connor."

He raised a brow at the familiar name. The boy looked around the right age. "I'm Mark. You don't happen to have a cousin named Sarah do you?"

Recognition shown in the boy's suspicious eyes. "You know Sarah?"

"We've met. I guess she was right about you." He released his hold on the delinquent, convinced he'd piqued the kid's curiosity enough he wouldn't bolt.

Connor crossed his arms. "What'd she say?"

"That you're a handful."

Pain dulled the eyes that suddenly dropped to study the ground. "I keep doing things that bug her. She's not used to having a kid around, and she is so boring." He rolled his eyes. "Plus her friends are awful! I can't stand them. They drink and talk all night long." He shrugged. "So I came out here to find something to do." He pointed toward the bike path. "Is that your dog?"

"Yes." He patted his thigh. "Sadie, come."

Sadie charged at them and bounded to a stop.

"She's friendly. You don't have to be afraid."

"I'm not afraid." He reached out a hand to Sadie and let her sniff it. "You're a pretty girl." He glanced up at Mark. "How old is she?"

"Three. You can pet her." He couldn't stop thinking about the boy's words regarding the women at his house. "You mentioned your cousin's friends drink too much. They don't hurt you, do they?" Mark's dad had been a mean drunk, and he had a short fuse for people who abused kids.

"No. They leave me alone. My cousin doesn't drink, and I can tell her friends' drinking bugs her, but she still lets them crash at her house." He shrugged. "Whatever. I guess she can't say no to family and friends. She doesn't like to hurt anyone's feelings. At least that's what my mom said about Sarah when she suggested I visit my cousin for the summer."

Mark hurt for this kid. He knew firsthand what it felt like to be unwanted and treated like a burden. "Did you want to come to Sunriver?"

Connor toed a rock. "I guess. I can fish, swim, float in the river, ride my bike and—"

"Scare tourists with water balloons?" Mark raised a brow.

The grin was all mischievous boy. "Yeah, that too. You're not going to tell Sarah, are you?" His voice cracked.

"Shouldn't I?"

"What if I promise to not throw water balloons for the rest of the summer?"

"You think you can keep your word?"

Connor nodded, sincerity in every bob. "Positive. My last one hit your stomach." A smirk stole across his face.

Mark rubbed his chin. "I suppose your cousin doesn't need to know about the water balloons. This could stay our little secret. But Connor," he waited until the boy looked up at him, "I'm a cop, and I don't want to see you get into any more trouble. Am I clear?"

Surprise and a hint of admiration covered the kid's face. "Yes, sir."

"Good. Now head on home before your cousin starts to worry about you."

Connor kicked a pebble with his sneaker. "Can I hang here with you? My cousin's friends are probably getting tipsy about now."

Mark sucked in a breath, and let it out slowly. This boy must really hate it at his cousin's if he'd ask to hang out with a stranger who happened to be a cop. He felt bad for him. He stared hard at the kid. If it hadn't been for Sam stepping up and getting involved in his life as a kid, he wouldn't be the person he was today. In fact, he'd probably be behind bars. Maybe Connor was his chance to pay it forward. "Sure, but you need to let Sarah know where you are. Is her place far from here?"

Connor grinned wide. "Two or three miles maybe. My bike is stashed over there." He pointed in the direction he'd been running when Mark caught him. "It's only fifteen minutes away from here when I ride."

"Okay then, grab it, and let's call Sarah." Sadie bounded ahead of them.

Connor walked his bike to Mark's house and rested it against the deck.

"Do you have a cell phone?"

The kid nodded and pulled a smart phone from his pocket and entered her number. "Hey Sarah, I'm at a cop's house."

"What!"

Mark could hear Sarah's panicked voice through the phone. He reached out a hand. "Let me talk with her."

Connor passed the phone to him.

"Hi, Sarah, we met earlier on the bike trail when you and your friends took a spill."

"Oh yeah. Sure. I remember. Why's Connor at your place?" Concern edged her voice.

He quickly explained, leaving out the water balloons. "Do you mind if he hangs out here for a couple hours?" He looked over his shoulder toward the boy who was swinging on the hammock and lowered his voice. "He sounds a little uncomfortable with your friends."

"Oh. Okay, sure. But, so you know, my friends leave Connor alone." Defensiveness edged her tone.

He'd believed the boy for the most part, but her confirmation made him feel better. "Connor said the same thing. I think he needs some guy time." Tension eased from his shoulders. His gut said these two were on the up and up, but he'd keep a close watch on the boy, to make sure. He'd been fooled before and didn't care for a repeat.

"That makes sense. Thanks for this. I can come by and get him at eight if that's okay."

"I'll make sure he gets home safely." He wanted to see for himself what Connor was going home to.

"Okay. See you in a couple then."

"Uh, one more thing. Please don't let your friends know I'm the one bringing him home." Even though he thought he could believe Sarah and her cousin, he wanted to see for himself that things there were okay. He didn't want the women to change their behavior because he was a cop.

She laughed. "No worries. Mum's the word. Thanks again."

Mark strode across the deck and handed the phone to Connor. He didn't care to see those women again, but his concern for the boy overrode any apprehension he felt. Best-case scenario they'd be in another room and wouldn't notice him when he brought Connor home.

"You don't like her friends either, huh?"

The kid was perceptive, but he wasn't going there with him. "You know what I don't like?"

Connor shook his head.

"Being hungry. Have you eaten?"

Sadie barked and sat facing him. Mark laughed. "You've eaten, girl."

Connor squatted beside Sadie. "I haven't, and I'm starving."

"How about burgers? I keep frozen patties in the freezer."

"Sounds good." Connor sat on the deck playing a game on his phone. Sadie curled in front of the hammock where Connor lounged.

Mark got busy preparing a bachelor meal for them and allowed his thoughts to drift through his day. Had he seen anything or anyone that might have been involved in the burglary? He'd met many people today, but the person that stuck out in his mind was the blonde. He shook his head. Nothing about her spoke trouble, except maybe the vehicular kind. He chuckled. She'd sure been irritated with him. She'd tried to hide it, but he could tell the woman was riled.

"What's so funny?"

"Nothing, just letting my mind wander. How's your game?"

"Okay. I used to play it all the time with my dad."

"Used to?"

"Yeah. He took off about a year ago, and we haven't seen him since."

"I'm sorry. Is that why you wanted to spend the summer here?"

The boy shrugged. "I think he left because of me."

Mark picked up the plate holding the burger patties and turned toward Connor. "I'm a pretty good judge of character. Even though I haven't known you long I can tell you're a great kid—a little mischievous. But I'd stake my reputation on this—you didn't drive your dad away."

"Thanks, but you don't know him. He never had time for me when he was around, and he always yelled at me." He shrugged. "I thought maybe if I wasn't home, he might come back. You know? My mom goes between being angry and sad. I want her to be happy again."

An ache penetrated Mark's heart. "It's obvious you care a lot about your mom and that you are trying hard to be a good son, Connor. Sometimes adults have problems, and even though it feels like it's your fault your dad left, it's not. That's on him, not you."

Connor looked at him with doubt-filled eyes. "You sure?"

"As sure as I am that my stomach is going to grumble if I don't eat soon."

A sad smile crossed Connor's face. "I like you, Mark. Even if you *are* a know-it-all cop."

Mark ruffled the kid's hair. "I like you too, even if you *did* hit me with a water balloon."

He took the burgers outside and slapped them onto the hot grill. The beef sizzled and smoke billowed up. He closed the lid and sat on a plastic chair, twirling the flipper in his hand.

What a welcome he'd had to Sunriver. He'd started the day getting run off the road, and ended it by getting reamed with a water balloon. What else did this summer of supposed rest and healing have in store for him? He was almost afraid to find out.

CHAPTER FOUR

THE FOLLOWING MORNING, NICOLE STEPPED ONTO the balcony of her room facing the golf course. She ran her hands up and down the goose bumps covering her bare arms, wishing the sunshine wasn't so deceiving. She hustled back inside for her sweater and checked the clock—six-fifty-five. Enough time to walk over to the café and meet Sarah.

Grabbing her bag, she slipped into flip-flops and made sure the door closed behind her. A wide meandering path led her to the café, where a large number of golf carts were parked. She dodged a cart and wove past a group of men sipping coffee and preparing for a morning on the links.

Too bad she didn't play. This place had to be a golfer's paradise with three championship courses and a great view of Mt. Bachelor from almost every hole—at least that's what the brochure in the lobby said. Based on the view from her room, she'd have to agree. The hum of a cart to her left drew her attention, and she stopped. The man from yesterday sat astride a bicycle wearing shorts and a polo shirt. Was that a police badge at his waist? Good thing he hadn't decided to ticket her. Looked like she owed him for that.

Nicole continued toward the café. Someone slipped a hand through her arm, and she jumped. "Sarah! You startled me."

"Sorry. I see you're as enamored as my friends were with that cop. He's a pretty nice guy, but not my type."

"*He's* the guy you and your friends were drooling over?" Yes, he was good looking, but he was a *cop*. Memories surged into the back of her mind that she quickly thrust away. She did not want to go there. Besides, he wasn't like those other cops, that much was clear. After all, he was only a bicycle police officer.

Sarah giggled. "Eavesdrop much?"

"It wasn't hard. I would have needed earplugs not to overhear." She smiled, hoping her new friend would find humor in her words.

Sarah grinned. "Don't worry. I won't hold it against you. So you like him too, huh?"

She shook her head. "It's not that." She glanced over at her new friend. "I was surprised to see he's a cop. We had a less than pleasant encounter on my way into Sunriver yesterday."

"Sounds interesting. I want to hear about this mishap." Sarah dragged her forward and inside the café. "But, after I get a caffeine infusion."

The idea that Sarah's friends were talking about that guy surprised her. She shook the thought away and studied the menu board. Plain coffee or a mocha? The smell of fresh coffee permeated the small space. Nicole breathed in deeply. This might very well become her favorite destination. A loud blender whirred—except for that horrible sound. Good thing seating was outside on the patio.

"How's your sunburn?" Sarah shouted as the noise stopped. The people around them sent a look their direction.

Nicole giggled. "Maybe we should wait to talk outside."

"Good idea." Sarah stepped forward and placed her order.

Nicole decided against a mocha and instead purchased a large coffee and a bagel. They strolled to the patio and found seats with a view of Mt. Bachelor near the open fire pit. Nicole squinted into the bright sunlight wishing she hadn't forgotten her shades.

"So how's the sunburn?"

"It hurts, but I'll live. I learned my lesson and bought a huge bottle of sunscreen last night along with the same stuff you sprayed on me."

"Good thinking." Sarah leaned forward and lowered her voice. "Don't look, but he's coming our way."

"Who?" Nicole swiveled in her chair and spotted the cop a few steps away.

"I said don't look," Sarah hissed.

Nicole quickly turned back and wrinkled her nose. "Sorry." Why was it whenever someone said not to look her first instinct was to do exactly that?

"*Shh!*"

"Good morning." He stepped between them, removing his dark sunglasses. He nodded to Nicole and smiled. "I see you found the lodge."

"Yes. Thanks." He wasn't nearly as intimidating when he smiled. Too bad they hadn't met under better circumstances.

He turned his attention to the other side of the table. "Hi, Sarah. Where's Connor?"

"Sleeping. Hopefully he'll sleep until noon and stay out of trouble until I get home from work. I can't thank you enough for bringing him home last night. My friends get a little rowdy, and I don't like leaving them alone in my home when they've been drinking."

"No problem. Connor will be spending the day alone?"

"Yes," She drew the word out, and her brow puckered. "He's almost thirteen. It's legal." Her voice hitched, as if she were uncertain.

Nicole watched the interaction between the officer and her new friend. Why was Sarah so tense? Had she had a bad experience involving the police too? *Ugh.* What happened to her brother was an accident, and she had to stop blaming the police. Grams had said as much many times through the years and she was right, but every time she saw one in uniform it reminded her of Robbie.

"I wasn't suggesting it wasn't. I'm concerned about him being alone so much. Mind if I check in on him?"

"I guess not." Sarah raised her cup to her lips.

"Good. I'll try to stop by this afternoon."

"I'm curious why you care so much about my cousin."

"Someone once took an interest in me, and it changed the course of my life. I want to pay it forward."

Nicole watched and listened to this complex man. Who was he exactly? One minute he was scaring a day of life out of her, and the next he was concerned for a kid's welfare.

He turned back to Nicole. "How's your vacation going?" He smiled, his eyes crinkling on the edges.

She stopped herself from gawking. Okay, so maybe Sarah's friends were right about him. And based on his concern for Sarah's cousin, he had a big heart too. "So far so good." She grinned—had she batted her eyelashes?

Sarah cleared her throat. "I'm sorry. I should have introduced you, but it looks like you've already met."

"Mark Stone." He thrust out his hand.

"Nicole Davis." Nicole's face warmed. His touch sent tingles through her fingers, and she pulled her hand away.

His lips tipped up in a sideways grin. "Well, I only wanted to say hello." He held up a water bottle. "I forgot to fill it this morning. I'm hoping the café will help me." His deep brown eyes held Nicole's for a moment before he waved and headed inside.

"I think he's into you," Sarah whispered.

Nicole shook her head. "No way. He was only being nice. Probably trying to make up for yesterday."

Sarah shrugged. "Whatever you say, but I saw a spark there."

"Speaking of a spark—you seemed to be uptight when he brought up your cousin. Everything okay?"

"I think so. I didn't want him calling Children's Protective Services on me for neglect."

"He wouldn't do that. Connor is old enough to be home alone."

"I know he is, but Mark already thinks Connor has a bad home life. I could tell by the look on his face last night when he brought him inside and looked around the room as if he expected to see a crime in action."

Nicole's eyes widened. "Really? Why would he do that?" Although she shouldn't be surprised, since cops were suspicious by nature.

"It's nothing." Sarah waved a hand before taking another sip. "So what are your plans while you're here? I'm always looking for someone to play tennis with."

Nicole refocused her thoughts. She was here to fulfill Grams' wishes. Period. Not get wrapped up in other people's drama. However, that didn't mean she couldn't enjoy herself while she was at it. "Tennis huh? It'd be fun to get in a few matches while I'm in Sunriver. But I'll warn you, I haven't played since my PE class in college."

"I'll go easy on you. When are you free?"

"I'm not sure. My grandma is more or less calling the shots." She needed to find the next clue.

Sarah looked around. "You talk about her as if she's still living."

Nicole shook her head. "Sorry. Grams passed away a month ago, and I guess I do talk about her as if she's still here. I kind of told you about this yesterday, but she was big on adventures, and it seems she thought I needed one. I have to follow the clues to see where they lead. Her last clue turned out to be a key, which led me to a property management company, Ponderosa something. When I leave here I'll be checking out of the lodge and moving to a house she rented for me." She still couldn't believe Grams had rented a house for her, but what was even stranger was that when she contacted the rental company they didn't have the next clue. Somehow she thought they'd have it. She needed to find that clue. The problem was, she had no idea where to look.

Sarah's face lit up like a child's on Christmas. "How fun! So that's what the key was for. Very cool. I actually clean the office at Ponderosa Home Rentals a couple nights a week. I suppose I should have recognized one of their keys from the key ring, but I really don't pay any attention to them."

"I thought you had another job."

"I do, but I'm a recovering shopaholic, and I need the extra money to help pay down my debt faster. Kind of a sensitive subject." She touched Nicole's hand. "I'm really sorry about your grandma, but that's about the nicest thing I've ever heard of anyone doing. She must've been one special lady."

Nicole's throat thickened. She took a slow sip of coffee, blinking away tears. A wave of longing fell over her heart. She missed Grams like crazy. If she spoke now, she'd start crying for sure. Sarah was right, Grams was very special.

Sarah's voice softened, a slight frown creasing her forehead. "Hey, are you okay?"

Nicole nodded. "Sorry. I still get a little emotional."

"I understand." She pulled a card from her wallet. "Give me a call when you know your schedule, and I'll reserve a court time."

"I will. Thanks." Nicole dropped the card into her bag, pleased she'd found a friend. It had been way too long since she could say she had a friend. She'd pushed all her old ones away with her work-driven lifestyle. At least here there was no danger of working too much, and she couldn't be accused of putting lesson plans or grading papers before her social life, like Justin, her ex-boyfriend, had accused her of. She had feared her time in Sunriver would be long, lonely, and boring, but things had changed. Grams had stepped this game up several notches from her past adventures. She'd be lucky to find the next clue and finish solving the puzzle or whatever the point was before summer's end. Could the house be the next clue?

CHAPTER FIVE

NICOLE PULLED INTO THE DRIVEWAY OF her new home-away-from-home. Who would have thought the last clue would have led to a house? The small home, probably made in the seventies, was painted in an earth tone that resembled the color of tree bark and had an attached single-car garage. Her stomach danced with nervous excitement. She slid the key into the lock then pushed the door open.

She caught her breath. A white leather couch faced a fireplace with a large flat screen television mounted above, and a cozy dining room with a banquet to the left of the main room connected to the kitchen. "Oh, Grams this is lovely."

She closed the door and stepped in further, breathing in deeply a fresh, warm, pine scent. Someone had recently aired and cleaned the house, giving the indoors the fragrance of the surrounding trees.

She rolled her suitcase across the hardwood floor, through the living room past the couch, and turned left toward the French doors and a deck enclosed by a tall wood fence. "I can't believe you did this, Grams." Leaving the suitcase, she stepped outside. Teak deck furniture and a gas grill filled the small space, perfect for a single person or a couple.

She spun around and headed inside, closing the doors behind her. Bypassing the kitchen, she found two bedrooms at the end of a short hallway. She grasped the railing of the tight winding stairs off the kitchen and carefully climbed them to the loft. Excitement grew with each step as reality sank in—not only did she get to spend the entire summer in her favorite vacation resort, she would be spending it in this cool little house.

The simple space held a floor to ceiling bookcase filled with tempting choices. A single recliner sat by the railing along with a floor lamp. *Absolutely perfect!*

A small folded piece of paper was taped to the chair. Her pulse quickened. She grabbed the paper and flipped it open.

Congratulations on following the clues that led to the house. I hope you are game for all I have prepared for you. Have you enjoyed your stay so far in Sunriver? Did you try the spa? If not, your skills are slipping, dear one. Keep your eyes, ears, and heart open so you don't miss another clue. Don't forget to bring along a good book.

The spa? A good book? Grams never wasted words in her messages. Somehow she'd missed the spa clue, but the book was definitely a clue. She flipped the page over hoping for clear instructions on which book. Nothing. Hmm. She went downstairs and dialed the lodge spa. "Hello, this is Nicole Davis."

"Ms. Davis, we've been expecting your call," a professional sounding female voice said. "Would you like to set up your appointment now?"

"Um, sure. What exactly am I having done?"

"You're pre-paid for a facial, manicure, and pedicure."

"Wow. Okay." She scheduled a time and hung up. Grams had thought of everything, but Nicole would give it all up to have her back. She swallowed the lump in her throat and marched to the master suite. The space, though adequate, lacked the posh feel of the rest of the house. It needed a makeover. The wood bedframe had multiple scratches, and the finish needed to be refurbished. The linens looked clean but were faded and worn. She turned and noted the dresser didn't look any better than the bedframe. At least the space appeared to be clean.

Midday sunlight streamed in through the large window. Voices traveled from the bike path not far from her home. She loved bicycling and was anxious for an excursion. The person at the rental office said that there were bikes in the garage. Trying not to run, she darted to a door that looked like it should lead to the garage. With a yank it swung open, but not without a loud squeak. A little WD-40 would work wonders on those hinges.

She flipped on the light. Two bikes, a blue tandem and a red cruiser leaned against the far wall. Excitement bubbled inside her, as if she was five on Christmas morning. She closed the door and walked over to the pair. Other than being well used they seemed to be in good condition. She pushed down on the red bike's seat — good.

Three helmets hung from a wall peg. She grabbed one that looked like it would fit and snapped it under her chin. It had been so long since she'd ridden the trails in Sunriver. After opening the garage door, she wheeled out and locked up the house.

Straddling the seat, she pushed off. *Wahoo!* The warm breeze lifted her hair, cooling her neck. The pine scent unfolded around her as her tires bumped over every rock and dip in the rough terrain. She finally made it through the stand of pine trees to the paved path and made a right toward the village. At least she hoped she was going the correct way. The circular nature of Sunriver's trails had a way of turning her around.

She slowed for a trio of bicyclists hogging the pavement and rang her bell. Relief washed through her when they moved to one side allowing her to pass. Riding that slow would drive her nuts. An annoying bead of sweat trickled down her back, settling at the base of her spine. She eased off the pedals to slow her pace and catch her breath.

Shifting down, she pedaled up a hill. Her thighs screamed at her to stop. She was more out of shape than she had realized. With one last thrust, she crested a hill and coasted. Her speed accelerated as she flew down the other side of the hill. Hair whipped in her face and across her sunglasses. She laughed, feeling true freedom. When was the last time she'd let loose like this?

She slowed at the bottom and couldn't help the smile that refused to leave. That was too much fun. She looked over her shoulder and sobered. Ugh. The old saying 'what goes up must come down' hit her like a brick. Going home would be a challenge. She'd probably end up walking instead of riding up the hill.

She slowed at a tunnel and maneuvered around annoying bars blocking reckless riders from speeding through.

"Excuse me."

Nicole's head jerked up and met the serious, but somehow friendly eyes of the handsome bicycle cop looking directly at her. She caught her breath and braked. "Hello again. Officer Stone, right?"

He smiled and stood, straddling his bike. "Feel free to call me Mark. And you're Nicole."

He pointed. "Didn't you see the sign?"

Walk bikes through tunnel. Nicole inwardly moaned. Why did it have to be *him* that kept catching her mistakes? Two times in as many days she'd failed to notice a traffic sign. Hadn't Grams warned her to keep her eyes open? She bit her lip and gave a tiny shrug. "Sorry. I had my mind on other things."

He grinned. "Maybe you could work on concentrating on what's in front of you instead of what's going through your mind." He teased. "It might make your life a little less dangerous."

She wasn't so sure about that since he was what was right in front of her. Of course, that's not what he meant. But she had no intention of letting him think she was concentrating on him.

Nicole got off and walked her bike over to him on noodle legs—she really needed to get into shape. "Unfortunately, neither episode has shown you the best of my driving and biking skills. I'm really not as dangerous as I appear, but I imagine we'll be running into each other all summer, so I hope I have the opportunity to prove my first impressions wrong."

He chuckled. "All summer? I thought you were a tourist. Didn't you say you're staying at the lodge?"

"I was, but now I'm in a house for the summer. Then it's back to real life." She dragged her eyes away from his gaze and motioned with her head. "I was on my way to the village."

"Have fun."

"I will. Thanks." With a wave she pushed off with her foot and pedaled away. Hopefully the next time she ran across Mark he wouldn't catch her doing something stupid like ignoring a traffic sign. She could go weeks at home without seeing a cop, much less engaging with one. This was definitely going to be an interesting summer.

MARK WATCHED NICOLE ZIP along the path toward the village. What was it about that woman that drew him? Maybe it was her indifference—or even more—did he detect a hint of insecurity that bordered on shyness? Or perhaps she was simply reserved. He couldn't quite put his finger on it, but he was intrigued enough to want to know more about her. "Nicole, wait up!" He pedaled hard to catch up to her.

She looked over her shoulder and wobbled to a stop. "What's wrong?"

Now that she was looking at him with her big green eyes, his mind went blank. He wanted to kick himself for his impulsive move. How did he tell her he wanted the pleasure of riding with her without sounding like a moron?

"Nothing. I thought … that is—" He motioned ahead. "You want company?"

"Um, sure." She gave him an uncertain look as she started pedaling. "Are you headed to the village?"

"No."

She gave him a sidelong glance, her face a mask of confusion.

He cleared his throat. "I thought you might like company. These trails can get lonely."

A small O formed on her soft looking lips, a knowing look on her face. Like she knew he was the one who wanted the company. She pushed off again. "How long have you been a cop?"

He kept pace beside her. "Ten years."

She glanced at him before focusing ahead. "Why are you working *here*? I'd think someone with that many years' experience would have a big city job at the very least. Not … this." She waved a hand toward his bicycle.

The surprise on her face almost made him laugh, but not quite. "In defense of bicycle law enforcement everywhere, there is nothing wrong with this assignment. That being said, I'm only here for the summer." He should probably have kept his mouth closed, but he'd already said too much. "I'm a detective in Portland. But I'd appreciate it if you'd keep that between you and me."

"Now *that* makes more sense. I can see you as a detective. Were you ever a patrol officer? Other than now, I mean."

"I worked my way up like every other detective. Tell me about yourself, Nicole. All I know is that you don't read street signs." He chuckled, hoping to wipe away the serious look on her face.

"In my defense I've been distracted. I'm actually a very responsible, rule abiding person. My grandmother considered me a workaholic, and I think she was right."

"Seriously? I don't see it." He winked.

"The responsible part or workaholic?" She sent him a teasing grin.

"Ha. Both."

"Not nice." A small smile tipped up her lips, but sadness claimed her eyes. "I'm on vacation, but believe me, were it not for my grandma, I'd be at home stressing about finding a job." She shrugged. "Last week I applied for every opening I could find."

"As a detective, I ran across a wide variety of people. Maybe I can hook you up someplace. What kind of job are you looking for?"

"Doubtful. I teach elementary school."

"I hear it's a tough market for teachers right now. Have you tried the Portland area?"

Her grip tightened on the handlebars. "You heard right, and no, I haven't. I prefer small towns to large cities."

"There are smaller school districts around Portland. Regardless, I'm glad you're here. Your grandmother sounds like a spunky lady." He eased in front of her and led the way around a jogger.

She pulled up beside him. "She was. I miss her a lot." A rock chuck dashed onto the path, stared, and then darted into underbrush. "Did you see that cute little guy?"

Was? He was thankful for the distraction. It sounded like her grandmother may have died recently, and he had no desire to talk about death. "Those little critters are all over Sunriver. But don't worry, they always manage to get out of the way."

"Why are you glad I'm here?"

"Huh?" He angled a glance her way.

"You said you were glad I'm here. Why? You barely know me."

He held in a grin. "Easy. Tourists keep me busy, especially the ones who don't read road signs."

She laughed. "I'm glad to help."

Mark almost did a double-take. What a gorgeous laugh. He'd like to hear that sound a lot more often. The village came into view. They followed the trail through the parking lot, and into the village. He braked, not wanting her to go, but not able to think of a good reason to stay with her. "Maybe I'll see you around."

"Probably so, since we keep running into each other." Her

eyes twinkled.

"Don't forget to walk your bike in the village." He couldn't resist teasing her.

Nicole tossed him a saucy look. "Yes, *officer*." Without a backward glance, she walked away.

Mark's pulse tripped into double time. He sure hoped their paths crossed, and soon. Nicole intrigued him, and he wanted to guarantee they'd see one another again, but he would need to tread carefully with her. She reminded him of a wounded animal, and he didn't want to cause her any more pain. Besides, he wasn't in a good place himself right now.

CHAPTER SIX

A BICYCLE FLEW PAST MARK, A boy crouched low over the handlebars. He blew his whistle. "Hey! Walk your bike in the village!"

The kid slowed to a stop, then looked over his shoulder.

Connor. A grin tugged at Mark's lips as he raised his hand and waved. "How's it going?" He wheeled his bike toward the boy.

Connor raised a shoulder. "Why do I have to walk my bike?" A hint of defiance brushed the words.

"It's the rule." He pointed toward a sign.

"It's a dumb rule."

Mark didn't care to get into an argument with the boy and shrugged off his declaration. "What are you doing today?"

"Riding. I wanted a soda, but I forgot my money."

"Come on, I'll get you one." They walked through the village until they came to the grocery store. Mark handed him a dollar and some change. "I'll wait with your bike, but hurry."

Connor took the money. "Thanks!" He darted inside.

Mark scanned the area around the grocery store and noted families as well as lone shoppers, some strolling and others rushing, probably missing the beautiful surroundings. Connor strutted outside with a root beer. He liked this kid and wanted more than anything to steer him in the right direction. The boy was at a critical juncture in his life and could easily go either way—the side of the law, or the side of those who break the law.

He recognized the rebellious look Connor wore like a neon

sign, had been there himself at that age, but at other times he glimpsed a child that only wanted attention and love.

"Here's your change."

"Keep it."

"Thanks." He pocketed the coins. "How much longer are you working?"

"Until five."

"Oh." Connor's shoulders slumped. "Sarah gets off at five too. She said we could play tennis tonight."

"What about her friends, Tina and Marge?"

"They left."

"That's good news, right?" Mark walked his bike back the direction they'd come with Connor beside him.

"Yeah. I have the house to myself now. No more nail polish, constant chatter, and the perfume—yuck." He rolled his eyes. "I hate the smell of that stuff!"

Mark chuckled. "Your cousin seems girly to me."

"Nope. Sarah is more of a tomboy. She's nothing like her friends."

"Odd they'd be friends with so little in common. Then again I have friends that are complete opposites of me."

Connor shot him a sideways glance. "Before Sarah became a Christian she was into partying. That's how she met the double-trouble-twins."

"Huh? Twins? They don't even look related."

Connor laughed. "They're not. It's my nickname for them. So what's with the blonde I saw you with? You like her or what?"

"Maybe, but we don't know each other well. I just keep running into her."

"My mom would call that fate."

Mark didn't respond. He had no intention of taking this branch of their conversation further.

"Where you headed?" Connor asked.

"Thought I might ride over to the lodge and around the golf

course. Want to tag along?"

His eyes lit with excitement. "Sure!"

Mark held back a chuckle with a cough. "If I have to deal with anything, you'll need to stay out of the way. Okay?" They came to the edge of the village, and Mark straddled the seat.

Connor nodded. "This is so cool! Wait until I tell my mom."

"Will she mind?"

"Nah. She'll think it's cool too. She's worried about me." He bit his lip.

"Why's that? She hear about the water balloons?" Mark teased as they rode slowly side-by-side.

"She thinks I'm becoming a," he scrunched his face, "hooligan. Her words."

Poor kid. He'd seen more than his share of kids labeled at a young age, and those labels too often stuck—or became prophetic. "Are you?" He liked Connor and didn't want him to subconsciously try to live up to the label his mother had given him.

"Nah."

"Good."

"Maybe you could play tennis with me and Sarah tonight."

"Thanks, but I don't think so." Nothing against Sarah, but he didn't want to give her any reason to think he was interested. Now Nicole, on the other hand, had something about her that drew him and piqued his interest. Too bad *she* wasn't the boy's cousin. Then he'd have a built-in excuse to spend time with her.

He'd have to find ways to be with Nicole without being too obvious and scare her away. Although she was friendly, he had a feeling one wrong move by him and she'd be history where he was concerned.

THE NEXT AFTERNOON, WITH freshly painted nails, Nicole left the resort spa and crossed through the parking lot to her car, shifting the large gift bag from one hand to the other. Sunlight glinted off the windshield of a parked car, blinding her for a moment. She stopped next to her car door and felt through her purse for her keys.

Grams really had her perplexed. She'd expected a note with a clue at the spa, but what she'd received left her confused—a black dress and slinky sandals, but no note. What was she supposed to do? Clearly Grams had planned something, but sadly she forgot to let Nicole in on her plan. Was the game over already? No, Grams always ended with a bang and usually a life lesson too.

"Hey there."

Nicole looked over her shoulder. "Hi, Mark. How's it going?"

He coasted to a stop beside her. "Fine. Is everything okay? You look troubled."

She held up the bag. "Another surprise from my grandma. Only this one I can't figure out. I wonder if I missed another clue?" She had run the last clue she'd found over and over in her mind, but nothing helped.

"Sounds intriguing. Maybe I can help." He rested his elbows on the handlebars and looked expectantly at her.

She shook her head. "Not unless you can explain what I'm supposed to do with a little black dress and sandals."

He cocked an eyebrow. "You don't know what to do with a little black dress and sandals?"

"She usually leaves a note or a clue of some kind."

He straightened and reached for the bag. "May I?"

She handed it over and watched him dig through it. "What are you looking for?"

"I thought maybe there might be something you missed, but it appears the clothes are the clue." He gave the bag back.

"I have the clue I found at the house. Do you think that might help?"

He shrugged.

She pulled it from her bag and held it out to him.

He unfolded the white sheet of paper. "'Congratulations on following the clues that led to the house. I hope you are game for all I have prepared for you. Have you enjoyed your stay so far in Sunriver? Did you try the spa? If not, your skills are slipping, dear one. Keep your eyes, ears, and heart open so you don't miss another clue. Don't forget to bring along a good book.'"

"What do you think?" Nicole reached for the paper, then tucked it back into her bag.

"It's interesting. Especially the part about a good book. Any idea if that part is significant?"

"Probably, but I have no idea which book she's referring to."

He shrugged. "She said to keep your heart open. Maybe she's hoping you'll find love or at least go on a date. And that's why she gave you the dress."

Nicole's cheeks burned. She should have thought of that. It sounded exactly like something Grams would do. Now she regretted letting Mark read the clue. How humiliating. "I . . ." How was she supposed to respond? Words escaped her. She looked everywhere except at Mark. How did she get herself out of this embarrassing situation?

Mark cleared his throat.

Her gaze swept to him.

He stared at his handlebars for a moment before looking up, straight into her eyes. "I clean up pretty good. If you're interested, *we* could get dinner together." He dipped his chin and raised a brow.

Nicole's heart pounded. Was he asking her out? What should she say? She'd never been skilled at relationships. Mark seemed like a good guy, and she didn't want to hurt him.

"What? Do I have a dead bug on my face or something?" He lifted a hand to his cheek.

She chuckled, grateful for the note of humor. "No. You just

surprised me."

"Oh. So, how about dinner?"

"Thanks for the offer, but to be honest I'm not sure it's a good idea."

"Why? I mean, I know we didn't get off to the best start, but I think we could manage to get along for an evening."

She took a deep breath and let it out slowly. "When you put it like that. I suppose I'm making a bigger deal out of this than it is. It's only dinner. Not a marriage proposal."

He laughed. "Nope. I'm not in the market for that."

"Good, because my ex-boyfriend said I'm terrible at the relationship thing." A flush crept across her face, and her heart beat a rapid staccato as lightheadedness washed over her. She swayed slightly and felt a hand on her arm. Her gaze traveled from the hand up the arm and rested on Mark's face.

"Are you all right? Maybe you should sit."

"No. I'm fine other than being embarrassed. I'm probably dizzy because I'm dehydrated and need to drink more water." She had to lighten the mood. She glanced around the parking lot and spotted a couple of kids near the Bike Barn. "I hear Connor is pretty taken with you. All he could talk about was you and how he got to ride along while you were patrolling the bike trail yesterday."

"You know about that?"

"Sarah called and invited me to join them for a game of tennis last night, and let's just say you made a lasting impression on the kid."

"He reminds me of myself at his age."

"You had a deadbeat dad and a mom that didn't have time for you too?"

He lifted a brow.

"Sarah told me a little about Connor's home life, and it's not pretty." She felt bad for Sarah's cousin but didn't really know how to help. It wasn't like a twelve-year-old boy would want to spend the day at the spa with her. But, maybe she could think of some way to ease the monotony of being alone all day. After all, she was a teacher; surely she could think of something.

"I only know that his dad left, and he blames himself."

Her breath caught. "I didn't know he blamed himself. That's sad. I wish I could help him, too. Any ideas?"

"Be his friend."

"Yeah." Easier said than done, but she'd make sure the boy had her number in case he needed something. "I should be going. And about dinner. Yes."

A slow grin spread across his face. "Okay. I'll be in touch." He waved, then pedaled away.

She watched his strong calves pump the pedals, power surging in each thrust. She pulled her gaze from him, slid behind the wheel of her Mini Cooper S, and tapped her fingers on the steering wheel. Would Grams really give her a knockout outfit with no place to wear it? Mark asked her out, but no way could anyone, including Grandma, have predicted that.

Jamming the car in gear, she backed out and zipped over to the village. A book she'd ordered awaited her, and she couldn't wait to spend the afternoon reading. She chuckled at the irony. Only a few days ago she'd been uptight at wasting time, and now this whole relaxation thing sounded like a good idea, especially after her conversation with Mark. She slid out of her car and quickly walked toward the bookstore.

A group of kids rested against the wall surrounding the mini golf course laughing and pointing. Someone must be providing them with good entertainment. She edged close to see what was so funny, but before she could get close enough the group scattered leaving one kid behind—Connor. "Hi there."

Connor whirled to face her. "Hey."

"What happened to your friends?"

He shrugged. "They aren't my friends. I was only standing here."

"Oh." Her earlier thoughts about the pre-teen flooded her

mind. She pulled a pen and a scrap of paper from her purse. "I wanted to give you my number in case you need anything while Sarah is at work." She jotted her number down and thrust the paper toward him.

"Uh, thanks." He stuffed it in his pocket and looked past her.

The unmistakable scent of waffle cones filled the air, giving her an idea. "I'm headed to the bookstore, but thought maybe I'd detour at the ice cream shop. Care for a cone? My treat."

His face lit. "Sure. Thanks!"

Nicole grinned. "Make it a single scoop. My pockets aren't deep." They walked side-by-side into the ice cream shop and stood in line. "What're you going to do until Sarah gets home today?"

"When I'm done here, I thought about fishing."

"Sounds like fun."

"You fish?"

"No, but I'd love to sit on the riverbank. That is, if you don't mind the company. I can read the book I was on my way to buy and you can fish."

"Why?" He narrowed his eyes.

"I'm here by myself for the summer, and I get lonely. What do you say? Can I hang out with you this afternoon?"

"Suit yourself."

It wasn't exactly an enthusiastic response, but she could tell by the gleam in his eyes that her company was welcome. They stepped up to the counter and placed their orders.

It looked as though Grams' game would help more than only her. Connor would benefit too. At least she hoped her company would be a positive thing. Wait until she told Mark she spent the afternoon fishing. She tilted her head in wonder that her thoughts immediately strayed to Mark.

CHAPTER SEVEN

MARK COULDN'T SHAKE HIS CONVERSATION WITH Nicole as he entered the police department. This game she was playing for her grandmother intrigued him. He looked around the bullpen and spotted Spencer.

The other officer stood at the counter pouring coffee, a scowl covering his face. It looked like the man had had a bad day. Mark grabbed a cup and filled it with ice-cold water. "Any more break-ins?"

"Not today." Spencer sighed. "I'm beginning to wonder if we'll ever get a solid lead."

"Keep digging. They always make a mistake. Have you looked into the renters? Maybe there's a connection there."

"Good idea." Spencer's eyes narrowed. "Catch you later." He strode off with a distracted air.

"Glad to help," Mark chuckled as he followed Spencer. The man was competent. Sure, he'd missed an obvious angle, but Mark believed Spencer would eventually catch the thief and hopefully sooner than later. His new co-worker was definitely in the zone. Maybe he ought to let Spencer see where the trail led without interfering.

He stopped and reversed course. He had his own issue to deal with—Nicole. So much for not complicating his life. Not that one date was a complication, and he could use the distraction, but he had a feeling she would become more than just a dinner date, and he wasn't sure he was ready for that.

Several minutes later Spencer walked over to him, his lips

twisted into a frown.

"What's wrong?"

"Another dead end. I called the property management company to check the rental history of the houses that were hit, and they were all rented by different people."

Mark arched a brow. "At least that's what it says on paper. Did the rental agency confirm the guests' identities with photo ID?"

"They're supposed to, but I didn't check." Spencer's frown deepened. He strode to his cubicle and booted up his computer.

Mark followed with new determination. With a little guidance, Spencer would make a good detective. "You checking the incident report?"

Spencer nodded. "I wish I'd been in on this from the beginning. I feel like I'm one step behind all the time."

"What happened?"

He shrugged. "Jenkins had a family emergency, so I took over the case."

"This your first big case?"

The younger man nodded.

Mark skimmed the report over Spencer's shoulder. It looked like they'd done a thorough investigation.

Spencer's phone rang and he snatched it up. "When? Okay. Tell her not to touch anything. I'll be there in five." He pushed back and bolted up. "Another house was hit and we have a victim this time."

Mark's adrenaline surged. "Mind if I ride along?"

Spencer's eyes narrowed. "You ever been to a crime scene?"

Mark bit back a laugh. "I have. I'm not as inexperienced as you assume."

Spencer nodded and moved toward the parking lot. "Good enough. Let's move."

Mark followed, then he strapped into the passenger seat of the cruiser. Was he making a mistake? He'd come here to recover from the bombing that killed his partner and to determine if he wanted to stay in law enforcement. Maybe his desire to get involved in this case was a sign he wasn't ready to give it up. Big city life didn't appeal right now, but this case drew him like an adrenaline junkie to skydiving.

Spencer pulled into the driveway of a small house and parked beside a familiar looking Mini Cooper.

Mark knew that license plate. His heart pounded. "I know the person staying here." He flung open the car door. "Nicole!" He took in the surroundings. Nothing looked disturbed. A false sense of peace enveloped the quiet cul-de-sac. Where was she? "Nicole!"

"Right here." She peeked over the top of the fence wall off the side of the house, ear buds hung from her neck, and she held an ice pack to the back of her head. He breathed easy for the first time since he spotted her car. A second later the gate opened, and she strode toward them. "I stayed outside like I was told." Her voice trembled, and her face was as pale as it had been earlier, when she looked ready to pass out in the parking lot.

He scanned her from head to toe, but held back from running his hands over her to assure himself she was okay.

"What happened?" Spencer glowered at her with his pen poised over a pocket-sized notebook.

Nicole inched closer to Mark. He gave her a reassuring smile. It took all his self-control to keep from wrapping an arm around her shoulder, but he settled instead for a hand on her shoulder. He glanced at Spencer. "Where's CSI?"

"We're it. I can process the scene if you want to interview Miss .. ?"

"Davis." Nicole pulled the icepack away from her head, then wrapped her arms around her middle. "How long will this take? I promised Connor I'd go fishing with him this afternoon. He's waiting at the river." Her voice caught and she pressed her lips together.

Mark lowered his hand and raised a brow. This woman was full of surprises. He looked to Spencer. "I'll do the interview."

Spencer shot him a knowing look and nodded. "I'll be inside." He slipped on a pair of blue latex gloves and entered through the front door that stood slightly ajar.

"Let's sit on the deck. I'll try to make this fast, so you can meet up with Connor." She didn't wait for his reply but headed for the gate. She held her body stiffly as if she was afraid someone would jump out at her at any moment. At least the knock she apparently took to the head wasn't bleeding, and at first glance she didn't appear to have a concussion.

He wanted to comfort her and tell her everything would be okay, but pushed his personal feelings aside and allowed his training to take over as he took in the scene. A grill and a metal table with four chairs and two lounge chairs filled the deck. Everything here appeared unharmed. Clearly the thieves weren't after patio furniture. He pulled his notebook and a pen from his pocket. "Do you have a list of the missing items?"

Nicole shook her head. "When I got here I found the front door open, but I remember closing and locking it. I figured the property management company was working inside. The first thing I noticed when I stepped inside was the missing television, which seemed strange because I hadn't noticed a problem with it. I closed the door and went into the bedroom then saw the TV in there was missing also." She paused. "I turned to check the other bedroom when someone rammed into me from behind, knocking me to the floor."

He lifted his eyes to meet hers. "How'd you get the bump on the back of your head?"

"When he ran into me, he hit me with something hard."

Mark made a note on the pad of paper he always carried in his pocket. "Did you get a look at him?"

She shook her head then winced. "No. I was dazed, and by the time I stood up he was gone."

His gut tightened. She'd not only been inside with the perpetrator, but she'd been assaulted. This burglary racket had just become personal. "You're lucky you only got a bump on the head. I'm glad you're all right."

"After he took off I called the management company. They told me to call the police."

"Most people would have called the police first." Mark rested his arm on the table.

She winced. "That's generally not my first instinct. The idea of calling 911 makes me nervous. But I managed."

His tension increased. Had something bad happened in her past to give her this feeling? "Why is that?"

"I don't know. I guess I wasn't sure it was an emergency since they'd already left. It bugs me so much when people call 911 for non-emergencies and clog the lines. I didn't want to be that person."

He nodded. Her excuse made sense. "You are one lucky lady. Did you see anyone else?"

She shook her head. "I can't believe it didn't occur to me that someone had broken in when the door was ajar. I've felt so safe here."

He wanted to lecture her for entering her house to begin with, but he stifled his professional impulse—she'd been through enough. "What about a vehicle?"

"And that's what should've clued me in right away it wasn't the management company. They always drive a truck with their logo on the side. There was a big van parked next door when I arrived, which I thought was weird because the whole cul-de-sac has been empty the two days I've been here."

This might be the break in the case they'd been looking for. "Can you describe the vehicle?"

"It was a white cargo van." Nicole wrung her hands together and her shoulders sagged. "I wasn't paying much attention, and I'm horrible with the make of vehicles. I can't even tell a Ford from a Chevy."

He didn't understand how that was possible. He'd always loved cars and had been able to identify different makes and models since he'd been a kid. "Okay. If you saw a picture of the van, would you recognize it?"

"Maybe. Probably not. I'm sorry, Mark. Cars and trucks aren't my thing. I can't even tell you what you drive except that it's black."

Mark chuckled. "Was anything else missing?"

"Not that I noticed." She shivered, in spite of the heat. "I can't believe they were in the house with me."

"They? You only mentioned one person. You think there was more?"

"Had to be." She said it matter-of-fact. "That was a large flat screen TV. I don't think one man could've carried it. It would have been too awkward."

He scanned his notes then looked up as Spencer came out the French doors. "I think that's all for now. Thanks for your help, Miss Davis."

"Sure." She looked at Spencer. "Are you done?"

"Almost." Spencer repeated a few of the same questions Mark had already asked. "Okay, that's it. You may go inside now. I don't think you'll have any more problems. It looks like they cleaned out anything of value. The management company will need to supply a list of missing items. What about you? Were any personal items taken?"

"I only had one suitcase and my laptop." Her eyes widened. "I didn't think to check."

Mark stood and touched her back. "How about we make sure nothing else is missing?" He followed her inside ignoring Spencer's arched brow.

She went straight to the master bedroom and opened the closet. "Whew. It's still here."

"You store your laptop in the closet?"

"I like to leave the blinds open and don't want anyone walking by to be tempted. So yes, I keep it hidden in the closet."

He chuckled at her challenging tone and raised a hand. "It worked—at least regarding your laptop. I'll need to remember that idea."

She grinned, then rifled through the dresser drawers. "It looks the same here." She turned and faced him then leaned against the dresser. "Guess they needed your expertise on this case, huh? I don't imagine the crimes in Sunriver compare to Portland."

He caught movement in his peripheral and turned. Spencer stood in the doorway with his arms crossed. Was his secret out?

"Anything missing?" Spencer leaned in and scanned the room.

"No." She closed the closet doors. "Thanks for coming so quickly."

"Just doing our job," Spencer said. He nodded his head toward the front door. "Let's move out." He strode outside, not waiting for Mark.

Mark turned to Nicole. "Are you going to be okay? You don't need to see a doctor for your head?"

"I'm fine. My head is throbbing, but it's nothing a pain killer won't fix."

He studied her pupils and noted she still had no signs of concussion. "Okay then, guess I'd better go." Although he didn't budge. "Call me if you need anything." He pulled a card from his wallet and wrote his cell number onto the back.

She nodded and took the card. "I should find Connor before he thinks I abandoned him."

"Good idea." He thanked God she was safe. Whether Spencer wanted his help or not, he was going to get it.

She offered a wobbly smile. "I'm glad you were the cop that responded to my call."

His insides warmed. "Me too." Her emerald green eyes

shone with trust. He didn't want to leave her here alone and hesitated. The fact that they were still inside when she entered suggested they weren't finished. Was Nicole in danger? "Do you have any place else you could stay for a few days?"

"Why?" Worry shot into her eyes.

He pressed his lips together.

"You think they'll come back!"

"I didn't say that."

"I'm outta here." She pulled a suitcase from the closet and proceeded to toss her stuff into it.

"Where will you go?"

"They can find me another house for the summer, and if not I'll demand my grandmother's money back."

"What about Connor?"

"I'll call him. Hopefully he'll understand."

"He's a smart kid. I'm sure he'll cut you some slack. I'll get in touch with you later." He wanted to stay, but Spencer was waiting. Mark turned at the door. "Lock the front door behind me." She instantly followed him to the door. He waited until he heard the deadbolt turn and then walked to the cruiser.

"Any time, Mark." Spencer called out the car window while tapping his watch.

"Sorry." He got in and buckled up.

Spencer stared out the windshield on the way back to the station. "Pretty lady."

Mark shot him a curious look. "I've noticed."

"You two seeing each other?"

"I asked her out for dinner earlier this afternoon." Mark wondered at the direction of the conversation. The man was clearly uptight about something, but he doubted it was his acquaintance with Nicole. "Is there a problem?"

Spencer cast him a sideways glance. "It strikes me as odd that this house was occupied, when none of the other targets have been. You mentioned checking into renters. Maybe Nicole is our perp, and she staged this to throw us off."

"What? That's nuts! I suppose she hit herself on the back of the head, too." Clearly the man was eager to point the finger at someone.

"Desperate people do desperate things. She had opportunity, and according to Miss Davis, none of her personal belongings were stolen. Seems suspicious. That's all I'm saying."

Mark worked his jaw. No way Nicole did this. He knew it in his gut, and it was never wrong. "Nicole is the victim. She said herself the missing television would've taken two people to carry. She didn't have anything worth stealing except her laptop, and I suspect they'd have taken that too if she hadn't come home and surprised them."

"Maybe. Or maybe she had help."

"No. It doesn't add up."

"Prove it."

"Prove you're right." Mark crossed his arms and stared through the front window.

"For a rookie you're sure cocky—especially a rookie at *your* age. Then again from what I overheard, maybe you think you're better than the rest of us. Because it seems to me you misrepresented yourself to the woman. She's under the impression you're an expert detective." Spencer signaled and turned into the station's parking lot.

Mark sighed. He never should've asked to ride along. "You make it sound like I'm ancient. I'm only thirty-two, and I didn't lie to Nicole."

"Sounded like it to me."

"Will you let it go?"

"Can't." He shifted and looked Mark in the eye. "Look, I don't care how you pick up on women, but don't lie about your qualifications to do it."

Mark ground his teeth. Keeping his past quiet wasn't worth this. "I said I didn't lie to her. I'm a detective in Portland. I've been on the force for ten years."

A slow grin spread across Spencer's face. "Now that wasn't so hard was it?"

"Huh?"

Spencer opened the door. "I already knew about Portland. But I wanted you to tell me. Sorry about having to use the woman to get you to confess."

"You baited me!" He reached for the door then hesitated. "So you don't believe Nicole is guilty?"

"It crossed my mind for about a second. But she doesn't fit the profile. She hasn't been here long enough to be our suspect."

Mark's shoulders relaxed, and a slow grin worked its way across his face as he shook his head. Part of him wanted to laugh, while another part of him wanted to give the guy a piece of his mind.

"Sorry about your partner by the way. I saw your file opened on the Chief's desk. I know I shouldn't have read it but couldn't help myself."

Mark's grin faded. He hopped out and crossed his arms. "You knew this whole time?" Annoyance mingled with anger toward the Chief. The man should've been more careful with his private information. "Who else knows?"

"Only me. I made sure to close the file." He cleared his throat. "Figured you wouldn't be able to resist this case. I hadn't counted on needing the help of your *friend* to get you involved though." He moved toward the station.

Mark ran around the car and followed. "Was this some kind of set up?"

"In a way. I thought you'd be an asset."

Mark shook his head, barely able to believe what he was hearing. He didn't know whether he should respect this guy for his ability to get to the truth or should be annoyed with him for being nosy and coercive. "So all this time you've been manipulating me to do exactly what you wanted."

"Pretty much." Spencer chuckled. "You had me worried. I was beginning to think you were going to turn in your badge at the end of the summer, but there's hope for you." He tossed the words over his shoulder. "I want your report on my desk within the hour. I think we're close. They messed up this time by hitting an occupied house."

"Yeah. Either that or they're getting braver." What if they started burglarizing houses regardless of occupancy? Mark sat at his assigned computer and got busy. Why had Nicole's house been hit when it was surrounded by vacant houses? His head jerked up. Why hadn't he thought to check that? Had they been robbed also?

CHAPTER EIGHT

FROM HER DRIVEWAY, NICOLE MADE A quick call to Connor, then tossed her suitcase into the car and peeled out of the street. No way would she stay there another night. Her only regret was leaving all the books she hadn't had time to read—plus there was still the *good book* clue she hadn't figured out. But it couldn't be helped. Grams wouldn't want her in danger.

She carefully navigated the road leading to the rental company. Maybe this was a sign that she should go home. She followed the curve of the road and then slammed on her brakes. A deer stood in the middle of the street. Lazily moving its gaze from her car, it meandered toward the side of the road edged by pine trees. Deer in Sunriver acted as if they lived in a zoo with no cares.

When Bambi had safely made it into the trees, Nicole pressed on the gas. What had the thieves been after? Mark and the other officer seemed unfazed by the whole thing. Probably been-there-done-that so many times a few missing TV's were no big deal. Well, it was to her.

She pulled up to the property management company and parked. Squaring her shoulders, she got out then marched inside. A man stood behind the counter in the sparsely furnished room. She rested her elbows on the counter. "Hi, I'd like to change houses."

"Is there a problem with the one you're renting?"

"Yes!" Her voice trembled. "I called a little while ago about a break in. I can't stay there anymore." She shivered.

The man ran his finger around the inside of his collar, and his face reddened. "Excuse me one minute please." He darted behind a cubicle wall.

Nicole heard whispering and walked toward the front plate glass window. Hopefully it wouldn't take too long to sort this out.

"Miss Davis." The man stood at the computer behind the counter and raised a brow. "I apologize for your experience." He cleared his throat. "However, you are staying in the home as a guest of the owner."

"What does that mean? I thought my Grandmother paid for the rent." She didn't know any homeowners in Sunriver. There had to be a mistake, unless Grams had a friend here.

"It means the owner is allowing you to stay for free this summer. If you'd like to switch houses I can arrange that, but there will be a rental fee."

Nicole sighed and her shoulders slumped. No way could she afford to rent here all summer. "That won't work. I'll check out and go home."

"But you can't!" Wide eyed, he wrung his hands. "Please, Miss Davis. Give Sunriver another chance."

"Not in that house. It's not safe."

"Begging your pardon, but any house can be burglarized. Besides, the chances of further trouble are slim. I'm sure you will be perfectly safe in the home provided you."

"I'd prefer to check out."

A woman stepped from behind the partition. She bit her lip and then seemed to make a decision. "Miss Davis, I was to only give this to you in case of an emergency, and I suppose this qualifies." She handed Nicole a small white envelope.

"Oh."

"Please read it before you do anything hasty."

Nicole nodded and ambled back to her car.

"Dear Nicole, if you are reading this, then I've failed. Please reconsider staying. Planning this adventure for you gave me such joy,

and I believe if you stick it out you will understand the importance of spending the summer in a place meant for fun and adventure. Please give an old woman one last request and stay.

I happen to know the owner very well, and she requested that you allow an interior designer to update the master bedroom and en suite. The owner trusts your judgment and wants you to make it the way you would want it.

Love, Grams

P.S. Have you found a good book on the bookshelf yet? Open it and enjoy."

There it was again. If she left the house, it would be impossible to finish the game. She owed it to Grams to finish, but what kind of person allowed a stranger to redecorate their rental? This was nuts! Her grandmother had done some crazy things before, but this topped everything.

The woman from the management company came outside and waved at her. "Miss Davis, I have something else for you." She approached Nicole's car and handed her a business card. "This is the company you are supposed to contact about the makeover. The owner has set a pre-paid budget."

Nicole took the card. "Belafonte and Son's Construction and Design." She looked at the woman. "You do realize this is crazy?"

She chuckled. "It is unusual, but enjoy it. An opportunity like this one is once in a lifetime."

"No kidding. So this is all legit? There isn't a hidden cameraman somewhere waiting to tell me I've been tricked?"

"I assure you. This is all on the up and up. Enjoy yourself and try to forget about what happened."

"Easy for you to say. You don't have a knot on the back of your head from the creep who broke into my rental." She sighed. "Okay. I'll stay, but I want new locks installed."

"Actually, maintenance is working on that as we speak." She handed her a new key. "If you will give them a couple of hours your place will be right as new by the time you return."

"Really?"

She nodded and grinned wide before turning toward the building.

"Thank you," Nicole called out as she set the letter on the passenger seat. "Grams, you have no idea what you're asking me to do." What about the burglars? What if they came back? Even though the chances of them returning weren't good, it still made her nervous. And the ache in the back of her head was a constant reminder of what they were capable of.

She closed her eyes, remembering the happy times her family had here when she was a young child before everything changed. Being in Sunriver felt right—at least until this afternoon. If she could get that feeling back, then this was where she wanted to be. She headed to the village since her rental was being worked on. She probably should've gone to the river, but Connor would only bombard her with questions she wasn't up to answering.

She needed to call the design company too. At least she had the book she'd purchased earlier and could lose herself in the story. Reading for pleasure had not been a priority for a very long time. In fact, taking time for any kind of pleasure had taken a backseat to life over the past several years. Between caring for Grams, finishing her Master's degree, and her first year of teaching, fun had become obsolete.

Nicole parked then snatched up her purse and book and tucked the business card inside to use as a bookmark. She got out, went into Brewed Awakenings, and purchased an iced coffee. Now where to sit? Outside was far more tempting. She found an open table and sat. The business card poked out the top of the book.

"This had better not be a joke," she murmured as she pressed in the phone number.

"Belafonte and Son's Construction and Design. This is Bailey."

"Hi. My name is Nicole Davis. I was given your business

card and told to call about a master bedroom and bath job."

"It's nice to finally put a voice with the name. We've been expecting your call. Would it work for you if Mrs. Belafonte and I come over to your home tomorrow to see the space?"

Nicole let out the breath she'd been holding. In spite of everything, she'd been half-afraid this was a horrible joke. "Tomorrow will be fine." They set a time and Nicole stuffed her phone into her purse. A tingle of excitement zipped through her in spite of everything.

She pulled out the thriller she'd heard great things about and tuned out the world around her. With care, she flipped to the first page while teetering on the edge of excitement in anticipation of the story. There was nothing like getting lost in a world of fiction.

Before long, she leaned back and stretched her legs forward, barely aware of the activity around her as tourists and locals strolled through the village. She reached for her coffee and was again reminded how much she liked this place. The book held her captive, and she flipped page after page.

"This is a surprise."

Nicole startled and looked up. "Hi, Mark." She moved her legs. "Want to sit?" He was out of uniform. Must've had a short day. She glanced at her watch and did a double take. She looked to her right. Long shadows shaded the plaza, and the air had cooled.

"Have you been here all afternoon?" He eased down into the chair beside her and crossed his ankle over his knee.

"Apparently." Where had the time gone? No wonder her back and tailbone hurt.

He shifted to face her. "I saw Connor out at the river."

"How was he? I hope he wasn't upset with me."

"He seemed as happy as any boy would be when the fish aren't biting." He shot her a grin. "He asked about you."

"Yeah. I probably should've kept my promise to him. It would have been a lot more comfortable sitting on the bank of the river, but I knew he'd have questions, and honestly I couldn't deal with that today."

He nodded. "I don't think he'll bother you too much. I told him as much as I could and that seemed like enough. He said if I saw you to tell you thanks."

"For what?"

"He said you'd know."

She shrugged. "I have no idea. I bought him an ice cream cone earlier. Maybe that was it."

"Maybe, but I think it had more to do with you taking an interest in spending time with him. I could tell he appreciated it."

His words eased her mind. "Thanks. Sarah is really concerned about him, and I wanted to do something to help. I wish it'd been more, but I guess the summer has just started, so there's time."

"There is at that. Where did they move you to?"

She rolled her eyes. "Nowhere. Can you believe the owner is gifting the place to me? I'd have to pay rent for another house or go home. A letter from Grams convinced me to stay. Plus, I had an interesting project drop in my lap." She told him about the room makeover.

"That's different. I'm glad you'll have something to distract you. I know what happened today really shook you up." He paused, looking at her, his brown eyes probing. "How're *you* doing?"

"Fine." She shifted, avoiding his gaze. She liked Mark, but he unnerved her at times. Like he could read her mind or something.

"Really? Most people don't sit in the village for half a day to read a book. You sure there's nothing you want to talk about?"

She sighed and set the novel aside. "I'm afraid to go back to the house." There. She'd said it. Truth was, when the woman at the property management office told her not to go back for a couple of hours it was a relief. Although staying away the entire afternoon had not been the plan.

He nodded. "I thought as much. I could check the place out before you go inside."

She blinked and nodded quickly. "Yes. I'd like that very much. How about I grab a couple of steaks from the grocery store and make us dinner? Unless you're a vegetarian. Then I could whip up eggplant parmesan or whatever you'd like." *Oh please say you'll stay.* She did *not* want to be alone in that house.

"Sounds great. I'm a steak kind of man. I'd actually stopped in the village on my way home from work to pick up groceries then noticed you on my way out." He held up a cloth shopping bag. "I can meet you at your place in say--thirty minutes. Will that give you enough time to shop?"

"Sounds about right." She bit her bottom lip. Could she stretch her shopping, so she didn't beat him to the house?

"All right then. Wait for me in the driveway." He strode toward the parking lot without looking back.

Nicole stood and tucked the book inside her purse before heading across the patio and inside the grocery store. The store was a mass of bodies and carts. She pushed a small cart along an aisle, tossing things in that she needed, then headed to the meat section and picked out two T-bone steaks. She wheeled her way through the throng of people to the produce section where fresh vegetables in various colors tempted her—she loved veggies. Salad and baked potatoes—sudden hunger made her mouth water at the thought. Ice cream finished off the list. Loaded with several bags she trudged to her car. Warm air whooshed out and smacked her in the face as she slid in.

She'd invited Mark for dinner. She already regretted the invitation. She wasn't exactly the greatest hostess. Her ex-boyfriend had made it abundantly clear he thought her inept in the relationship department. But Mark was only being nice—there was nothing between them, so no need to stress in that area.

A short time later, she pulled to a stop in her driveway and rested her hands on the steering wheel as she stared at the house.

Tingles zipped through her body as her heart raced. She wiped her damp palms on her shorts. Could she really go inside after what had happened?

The house looked peaceful with no sign of the break in. It was funny how things could appear normal, when reality was so different. Glancing at her watch, then the rearview mirror, she scanned the street. Mark would be here any minute. Maybe it'd be okay to go inside. Sooner or later she'd need to be able to come and go on her own. There wouldn't always be a knight in shining armor to protect her. Besides it was still warm enough out that the ice cream would turn to soup if she waited out here too much longer. She took a deep breath and let it out slowly. "I can do this." If she was going to continue living here, she had to be brave and face her fear head on. A sound coming from the deck made her jump.

MARK SNAGGED THE CELL phone off the kitchen counter on the third ring. "Hey, Spencer." He scooped dog food into Sadie's bowl and set it on the kitchen floor.

"Glad I caught you. I might have a lead in the case. You want to meet me at the station?"

Mark rubbed the back of his neck. He was due at Nicole's in ten minutes. "Okay, but it'll have to be quick. Can you fill me in now?"

"Nope. This you gotta see."

With her food dish now empty, Sadie stood at the back door waiting to be let out. Mark slid the door open and she bounded off the deck. He'd meet up with her in front. He grabbed his keys and hustled to his car with the phone still pressed to his ear. "I can stop, but I'm in a hurry, so it'll have to be quick." In reality, he didn't have any time to spare. Hopefully this would be worth the delay.

Sadie rounded the corner to the house and hopped into the car when he opened the door. The station was out of his way, but if this would help put the people who hurt Nicole behind bars then a few extra minutes were worth it.

"What's the rush?"

Mark explained his plans for the evening.

Spencer chuckled. "Man you sure don't waste time."

"Let it go. It's not what you think. She's scared, and I'm trying to help her feel better."

"You do that for all the victims in the cases you work?"

"No." He'd connected with Nicole outside the case and considered them friends or at the very least acquaintances.

"You have a smart phone?"

"Yeah."

"Okay. I'll send you what I have. That way you won't have to come here. Let me know what you think."

Mark disconnected the call and pushed the twenty-five mile per hour speed limit to reach Nicole's place. He might make it on time. A short while later he pulled up beside Nicole's empty car. Where was she?

His pulse kicked up a notch, and he cut the engine. He ran to the door and raised his hand to knock.

The door swung open, and Nicole screamed. "You scared me! What are you doing standing here?"

"What are *you* doing inside? I thought you were going to wait for me."

Her chin lifted, and fire smoldered in her eyes. "I was, but then there was a sound on the deck, and it scared me. I couldn't stand not knowing what caused it. Turned out to be a squirrel, and I realized how silly I was behaving so I went inside. Plus I bought ice cream and didn't want it to melt." Her face softened. "Sorry. I'm still a little jumpy, but I knew you'd be here any minute." She brushed past him and strode toward her car. "I didn't hear you knock."

"That's because I didn't get a chance." He sidled up to her as she opened the door. One bag sat inside a plastic crate on the back seat. "I can get that."

"Thanks." She waited for him to grab the bag. "I hope you're hungry. I have a feast planned." She stopped. "Is that your dog?"

Sadie sat beside his car.

"That's Sadie. I hated to leave her home since I've been away all day. Do you mind?"

"Not at all, but she has to stay outside. I don't think the rental agency allows pets."

"No problem. She can hang out on the deck." He whistled for his dog.

"She's beautiful."

"Thanks." He squatted and scratched Sadie's back. "She's a good girl." He stood and opened the gate to the deck. Sadie sniffed the deck then stepped into the area as if it was home. "I think she likes it here."

"We can go in that way too." Nicole stepped past him, then moved toward the French doors. She waved a shaky hand toward the kitchen as she led him inside.

Interesting. It looked like she was more nervous than she let on. "Did you still want me to check things out and make sure we're alone?"

Her eyes widened. "If you think it's a good idea."

"It can't hurt. Wait here." He moved to the hall and looked in the bathroom—clear. The bedrooms were clear as well. He checked all the closets and under the beds then up in the loft. "No one's here besides us." He turned and she bumped into him. He grasped her shoulders to steady her. "Whoa there."

"Sorry, I didn't like waiting at the door. It gave me the creeps. Which is nuts since I came in on my own earlier, and I had Sadie with me, but when *you* thought you should check the place out, I got creeped out again."

He lightly squeezed her shoulder. "Relax. I think you're perfectly safe. Whoever was here earlier is long gone. I'm sure you have nothing to worry about anymore." He never should've planted a seed of doubt in her mind. It was just him being overly cautious and borrowing trouble.

"That's what they said at the property management place too. Speaking of which. They brought over two new television sets."

"Now that you mention it, I did notice the new TV's. They move fast."

"Yeah. I think they were trying to make me feel better about staying here. They replaced the lock on the doors and cleaned the house too. It was nice walking into a fresh and clean smelling place again."

His phone vibrated, indicating an incoming text. "Hold that thought. I need to check something on my phone. Be right back." He opened the French doors and stepped onto the deck with Sadie at his side as a woodchuck scurried across the planks then hopped onto the dirt below, staring at him as if offended. "Leave it," he said to Sadie as he pulled out his cell and accessed the info Spencer had sent. It looked like Nicole's place hadn't been their lucky break like he'd hoped. He pressed in Spencer's number. "Hey, I have the picture. Any chance the plate can be enhanced?"

"It's doubtful." Spencer sighed. "Did you notice the deer is blocking the license plate?"

He pulled up the picture again. "Good point. At least we know the make and model."

"We got lucky the bicyclist came forward with this photograph. Apparently he rides around snapping shots of nature all over Sunriver and said he had a bad feeling about the vehicle when he saw two men carrying a large screen TV out to it, so he snapped the shot."

"Too bad he didn't get the men in the picture."

"No kidding. I asked him to let me look through his

collection in case he inadvertently caught the thieves elsewhere."

"Good." Footsteps tapped on the deck. He looked over his shoulder. Nicole held a plate with two thick steaks piled on top. "Give me a call if anything else turns up." He pocketed his phone.

She pressed her lips tight and studied something beyond his shoulder, then her eyes locked with his. "Do you think the thieves will return?"

CHAPTER NINE

NICOLE GAZED TOWARD HER RENTAL HOUSE from her seat on the deck and unease gripped her, even with Mark inside the house checking out the new TVs. This summer was turning into a rollercoaster of emotions, and right now it was a nightmare. If Grams hadn't been so insistent she not leave Sunriver, she'd be safe at home right now. Instead, she was scared and alone. Well not exactly alone, but Mark would eventually leave and then she'd be alone. Mark couldn't assure her she was completely safe here. No one could. What if the burglars came back? Sure, it wasn't likely, but no one could guarantee they wouldn't return. She shivered.

She opened the grill lid, wincing at the loud squeak. Using tongs, she placed the steaks onto the hot rack. The aroma from the sizzling meat made her mouth water.

"Those are nice TVs. I wish my rental had an up-to-date television." Mark stood in the doorway.

She jumped as the timbre of his voice broke the quiet of the evening and hoped he hadn't noticed. Her hands clutched the tongs until the metal pinched her fingers.

He walked over and placed a gentle hand on her shoulder. "You need to relax. I know you're concerned the burglars will return, but all the evidence points to a simple break-in. You aren't the target of some big crime ring. The rest of your summer should be uneventful." He gave her shoulder a gentle squeeze. With a tender smile, he closed the lid and removed the tongs from her hands. "Maybe I should take over from here." He gently steered her to one of the deck chairs. "Be right back." He strode inside and came out with tall glasses of iced tea.

His touch did strange things to her stomach. Butterflies threatened to burst from within if she didn't get this silly school-girl infatuation under control. That was all it was. He had helped her, and now she was drawn to him.

"What's the frown for?" Concern etched his eyes.

She shook her head. "Sorry. I'm letting my mind wander to a place it shouldn't go. I feel a little better knowing it was a random break-in." She tried to give him a confident smile. "I'll be back in a minute. I left some stuff inside."

He followed her. "What can I bring?"

She handed him a tray piled with tableware. "I'll gather the rest and be right behind you."

She quickly assembled the salad, condiments and potatoes she'd nuked in the microwave and placed them on a second tray, then hustled after him. "You're sure I don't need to worry about the burglars anymore. Right?" Her fingers grasped the tray in a tight hold.

He set placemats on the table. "As sure as I can be. There's no reason to believe differently." He leaned toward the grill and breathed in deeply. "The steaks smell great. You mind if I check them?"

"Not at all."

He lifted the lid and his deep blue T-shirt hugged his biceps. The lid gave a loud squeak and he winced. "This thing could use a lube job."

"Yeah. It's kind of obnoxious." She pivoted. "I forgot iced tea to refill our glasses. Be right back." She grasped the pitcher containing amber liquid then returned to the deck. She lifted the lid and a puff of smoke greeted her. With the tongs, she placed the steaks on a serving platter.

"Looks good." Mark said from close behind. His warm breath tickled her neck.

Glancing over her shoulder, she caught her breath at his nearness. His lips were close enough to kiss if she moved ever so slightly. *Ack!* She needed a timeout. She handed him the platter. "Be right back. I forgot knives." She slipped past him then rushed inside to calm her racing heart. She could not allow Mark to have this kind of effect on her. A moment later, confident she was in control of her emotions, she grabbed the knives, then strode back to the table.

Mark rubbed his hands together and eyed his steak. "This looks amazing." He eased into a chair at the table.

"It better be." She grinned, sat beside him, and offered him the salad bowl.

He placed it beside his plate. "You mind if I offer a blessing?"

"Not at all." She closed her eyes and bowed her head.

"Thank you, Lord, for this meal. May it taste as good as it looks, and please be with Nicole and give her Your peace. Amen."

Peace was exactly what she needed. "Amen." She placed a napkin in her lap and dug in.

"Have you found any more clues from your grandma?"

Nicole shrugged. "Only if you count a note that implored me to stay and not go home. Oh, and that clue about a good book is still stumping me." She fingered her napkin. "I wonder if the book is special to one of us. Maybe one she read to me when I was a child. I feel like I should know what she's talking about. It must be in this house though."

He rubbed his chin. "Have you looked?"

"Not much. I need to scour through the bookshelf, but with all that's been going on, I haven't taken the time." She cut at her steak. "I know, I know. If it's a clue, the game will be stalled until I find it, which more than likely is in the book."

He frowned as if in deep thought. "How would she know what books are in this house unless she put it there herself?"

Nicole shook her head. "She was too sick to have done that. Besides, I was her caretaker. She couldn't have taken off for a day without me knowing." She tapped her fingernails on the plastic table. "Unless . . ."

"What?"

"Well, I had to go to an out of state training last summer for a few days. She was doing pretty well then, and I felt comfortable leaving her alone. Do you think she could have done all of this last year?"

"It's possible. I assume she knew she was dying."

"Yes. She actually lived longer than her doctor expected. Grams was very good at planning treasure hunts. But if she didn't come last summer then I'm sure she had help."

"What about your parents? Could they have been in on it?"

Nicole shook her head. "Not a chance. Grams was my rock. She was always there for me and always made sure I went to church when I visited her."

"I think I would have really liked your grandmother." He leaned forward resting an elbow on the table.

"Not if she caught you with an elbow on the table." She grinned. "Oh my goodness, she was a stickler about manners. When I was a kid, I always had to ask to be excused from the table or else . . ."

He chuckled and removed his elbow from the table.

"I almost forgot. An interior designer is stopping by tomorrow. The owners of this house want a master bed and bath makeover and want *me* to decorate in my taste. Isn't that the craziest thing you've ever heard of?" She took a sip of her tea. "Unless I know the owner. Clearly they knew Grams. That must be it. They know me, and that's why they asked me to give my input for the makeover."

"Makes a lot more sense than a stranger. Plus since your Grandmother did all of this, it fits that she'd be friends with the homeowner." He grinned. "One mystery solved."

"But I wonder who owns this house."

He laughed. "Why not let them stay anonymous? Clearly

that's their desire."

She shrugged. "Good point. Besides, I have enough to figure out without adding one more piece to the puzzle. I'm stalled with Grams' game and need a jumpstart."

"Maybe you should retrace your steps, so to speak, and re-work your way through the clues you've received so far. You could have missed something that will guide you to the correct book. If you need any help, I enjoy solving puzzles."

"I should hope so since you're a detective. I'll let you know. Your idea to backtrack is a good one. First thing tomorrow I'm going to do that."

"Any idea what your grandma had in mind when she planned your treasure hunt?"

"As far as the end game goes—no. But I have a strong impression she wants me to relax and have fun this summer."

"You don't normally enjoy life?"

She did laugh this time. "I've been too busy for the past seven years to enjoy anything. I finished my master's with honors a little over a year ago, then taught for a year. I guess you'd say school has consumed my life."

He forked a bite of steak into his mouth and chewed slowly.

"Now I'm unemployed and looking for a new position, thanks to budget cuts."

"What grade do you teach?"

"Fourth, but at this point I'd take any job from third to fifth. I applied to all the openings I could find in Oregon's smaller towns, but my résumé is scant, so who knows."

"That's something to pray about. I'm sorry you're going through so much right now."

"Thanks. And thanks for reminding me to pray. I'm afraid I haven't given the Lord much thought in a while." She studied her glass. Maybe her visit to Sunriver was about more than relaxing. She was glad Mark had reminded her to pray.

"You're welcome. It's funny how sometimes the last thing

we think to do is take our problems to the Lord, when talking to Him should be the first thing we do. I couldn't do what I do without my faith in God. It's what gets me through each day." Mark dug into his potato. "This is great by the way."

His conviction intrigued her. What made this man tick? "How? I mean how does your relationship with Him make a difference? Especially with being a cop and all that you see, I'd think you'd question His existence, not believe He's always there."

Pain flashed in his eyes, and he touched his chest. "I know it in here because He's helped me through some tough stuff I never could handle on my own." His voice softened. "I still have a way to go, but He's helping to sort out all the garbage that has happened recently."

"Like what?"

MARK QUIETLY TURNED HIS glass around and around then finally met her gaze. "A bomb killed my partner not too long ago. It really messed me up." He swallowed the lump in his throat. "I wanted to retire from the force, but my boss convinced me to take the summer and think it over. He encouraged me to take the job here. He thought the setting and change of pace would help me gain perspective."

She reached over and covered his hand, then quickly snatched it away as if she hadn't meant to touch him. "I'm so sorry. That must've been awful. Were you there?"

He nodded. "Yes, sort of." But not near enough to make a difference. He closed his eyes, as the scene replayed like a movie in slow motion. "Tracy was in a rush and didn't wait for backup. She was always in a hurry. I was seconds behind her. I tried texting her . . . even calling her, but she didn't have her cell phone." When he got to the scene, he'd called out to her to stop before she picked up the bag, but it was too late. He squeezed his lids tight. He knew it wasn't his fault, but the guilt still plagued him. If he'd been there a little sooner, he could've warned her to not touch the bag. "I tried to stop her." His voice sounded strangled. He needed to get a grip. It wouldn't be pretty if he lost it, and Nicole didn't need to see that.

Laughter from the direction of the paved path invaded the moment. He blinked away the memory. Nicole's watery eyes twisted his gut. He cleared his throat and stood. "Want help cleaning up?" He swept up several dishes, then fled into the privacy of the house.

Standing at the kitchen counter he flexed his shaking hands, trying to regain control. He hadn't shared that with anyone outside the official inquiry. It still felt fresh, like it'd just happened. Tracy bending toward the bag was forever imprinted in his mind's eye. Would the horror ever go away? He'd thought he'd started to win over the emotional torture, but talking about it had brought everything back in full force. *Lord, please help me get past this. I need Your peace.*

Everyone had patted his back and reassured him that there was nothing he could've done. But he couldn't help feeling responsible. They were partners and had each other's backs, but he'd failed. His one source of comfort was knowing she was a Christian and in heaven. If not for that . . .

"I'm sorry about your partner." Nicole's voice sliced through the quiet kitchen. "You said you were nearby when the bomb went off. Were you injured?"

"Minor injuries." He turned to her and offered a weak smile. "God has helped me a lot. I was a mess right after it happened. I've come a long way."

"You sure it wasn't you helping you? No offense to Him intended." She gave a quick glance upward. "But it seems to me you're a resilient person, plus you're clearly still dealing with this tragedy."

"True, but according to the book of Isaiah, He gives strength to the weary."

She nodded and pursed her lips.

It seemed his new friend had some faith issues. "There's a church here in Sunriver. Now that you're taking time to enjoy life, maybe you'd like to join me on Sunday."

"I haven't been to church since Grams' funeral. I'll think about it." She set down the tray she'd been holding. "You up for dessert? I have ice cream."

He should probably go home, but she clearly wasn't yet ready to be alone. "My favorite."

She dished up two bowls and led the way to the couch. They talked for hours until Nicole looked at her watch and gasped. "I can't believe it's ten o'clock. I'm sorry for keeping you so late." She jumped up from the couch. "Thanks for coming over tonight."

"It was my pleasure. I know I said I'd be in touch about our dinner date, but in spite of all that's happened . . . the offer stands. I'm free tomorrow night."

"Okay. I'd like that. But as friends, not a date, and I'm paying for my own meal. I like you and don't want to mess up what we have with romantic entanglements."

He chuckled. *Romantic entanglements?* "I can live with that."

"You're different from what I expected after our first encounter. Honestly I was a little afraid of you when you stalked toward my car. And when I saw your huge biceps I thought . . . well never mind what I thought."

"You thought I was going to hurt you?"

"Kind of. But only at first," she quickly added.

He enjoyed lifting weights, and his strength had come in handy more than once on the job, but it bothered him that she'd been afraid of him. He cleared his throat. "Okay. I'm glad it was only at first. I'll pick you up at six for dinner tomorrow." He glanced past her shoulder toward the kitchen. "You want help washing the dishes?"

"No thanks. I'm an obsessive-compulsive cleaner."

He lifted a hand and backed up with a grin. "No, not that."

She walked with him to the front door.

"Don't forget to lock up." He tapped the door as he stepped outside. "I'll get Sadie and be on my way."

"See you tomorrow night."

Mark turned toward the deck gate but stilled before retrieving his dog, listening for the sound of the lock to fall into place. A grin tipped his lips. Tomorrow night would be interesting. He got Sadie settled then put his car in gear and headed to the PD. Unless he guessed wrong, Spencer would still be around, and he wanted to check in and see if he'd found anything in those other photos.

At the station he left Sadie snoring softly on the backseat, then he found Spencer still clicking through pictures on his computer. "Figured I'd find you here. How's it going?"

Spencer looked up with tired looking, red eyes. "Nothing. I guess now I understand why the guy questioned me when I said I'd like to see all his pictures. There must be several thousand on this file."

"He took all of these in the past two weeks?"

Spencer nodded.

Mark rubbed his neck and returned his gaze to the screen. "Want help?"

"Please. I could use a break. If I see one more deer or bird, I may go cross-eyed." Spencer stood and stretched.

Mark chuckled and slid into the seat Spencer vacated. "You should go home and sleep."

"So should you, but you're not either. How was dinner?" A teasing lilt accompanied the question. Maybe Spencer wasn't *that* tired.

"Great." He rested his hand on the mouse and clicked through to the next picture before glancing at Spencer.

Spencer waggled his brow. "Sounds like you did more than put her mind at ease."

"Easy, man. I don't like your insinuation."

Spencer's neck reddened, and the grin slid from his face. "Sorry. So what'd you eat?"

"What's with all the questions? You hungry or something?"

"Yeah. Think I'll go grab a bite. Be back in thirty."

Mark waved him off and clicked through the photos until one caught his eye. In the background, a white van sat in front of a house. He enlarged the photo to see the address on the house and cross-referenced it with the houses that had been hit. "Bingo." But like before, the license plate wasn't visible.

He clicked to the next picture. One of these may very well hold the key to solving this puzzle. His cell phone buzzed in his pocket. He glanced at it and answered. "Nicole, what's up?"

"There's a white van in the driveway across the way from my house," she spoke quietly, but the panic in her voice rang clear.

His heart rate spiked. "Stay inside and double check the locks. I'm on my way."

CHAPTER TEN

MARK PHONED SPENCER AND MET HIM in the parking lot.

"Get in, I'll drive." Spencer flipped on his light bar and tore from the lot. "You think it's our guys?"

"No idea, but it's a white van, and Nicole said no one has been around." He'd practically promised Nicole she was safe and now this. It didn't make sense that they'd go back to the same neighborhood after nearly being caught at Nicole's house. What was up with these guys? Clearly they weren't easily deterred. *Please keep Nicole safe, Lord.* They had to stop these guys before someone got hurt.

Spencer accelerated.

"Take it easy. If we crash on the way, it won't help anything."

Spencer eased off the gas as he rounded the next circle, then accelerated into the straightaway. A minute later they pulled into the cul-de-sac and slid to a stop behind the van, leaving the lights on.

A man stepped out of the house, his eyes widened when he spotted the police cruiser. "What's going on?"

"Do you have I.D.?" Spencer asked.

"In my wallet. It's in my back pocket."

Mark poised his hand by his side ready to draw his weapon if necessary. He may not be in uniform, but he still carried a sidearm.

"I rented the house for seven days. Is there a problem?" He handed his driver's license to Spencer.

"Be right back." Spencer strode to his cruiser and called in the information—standard procedure required they run a check on the truck and the driver.

"Where are you from?" Mark kept an eye on the man and the door that stood open.

"Albany. My wife and I like to get over here at least once a year."

"Is your wife inside?"

"Yes. She's unpacking. We got a late start and arrived a short time ago." He shot a look toward Spencer then returned his attention to Mark. "What's going on? Is there a criminal on the loose or something?"

Spencer sidled up to them. "Sorry to bother you Mr. Clint. Someone called in a suspicious vehicle."

"Oh, okay. No problem." Relief covered his face. "So there's no dangerous criminal in the area?"

"Everything is fine. Enjoy your stay," Spencer said.

Mark followed Spencer and slid in the cruiser beside him. "Well?"

"The owner of the rental agency was not happy to have been awakened from a sound sleep, but he was cooperative. Mr. Clint and his wife are registered guests. Apparently he and his wife rent this house every year this exact same week." Spencer pulled out.

Mark pressed in Nicole's number. "You can rest easy. He's a tourist, nothing more."

"Oh good. I'm so embarrassed."

"Don't be. You did the right thing."

"Okay. Thanks. See you tomorrow."

Mark pocketed his phone. It'd been a long day, and he was ready for it to end. Tomorrow he'd look at this case with fresh eyes. They had to be missing something.

THE STATION BUZZED WITH early morning activity as officers changed shifts. Mark sidled up to Spencer's desk. "Anything new?"

"Maybe. I need you to work tonight."

"Why me?" He crossed his arms. Surely another cop was available. He kept his voice low. "Spencer, you're killing me. You know I have a date."

Spencer shrugged. "Sorry, but you're by far the most experienced investigator we have, and these break-ins have to stop. The Home Owners Association is demanding answers that I don't have, and I'm sick of fielding calls. Besides that, it's infuriating that we haven't caught these guys yet."

"I understand, but can't it wait a couple hours? It's not like this is life or death."

Spencer looked around the room and motioned him into a nearby conference room then closed the door. "Look, I don't know who the players are in this, but since it all began before you got here, I know I can trust you."

"Are you suggesting cops are involved?"

Spencer shrugged.

He kept his voice low. "Do you have a credible reason to believe a cop is involved?" He hadn't been in Sunriver long and really only knew Spencer well.

"No, but the fewer people who know, the less chance that someone will accidentally reveal information they shouldn't."

"Okay. I'm listening." Mark leaned against the conference room table and wished the Sheriff's department had this case, rather than their tiny police force.

"I received a tip that needs follow-up. I don't know what I'm stepping into and need backup."

This changed things. Mark couldn't turn his back on a fellow officer. "That's all you had to say. Fill me in."

"There's supposed to be another break-in tonight." He shared the address.

Mark's gut clenched. "That's on Nicole's street. What is it about that cul-de-sac?" He'd assured her she was safe and now this.

Spencer nodded. "Makes you wonder huh? So far all the break-ins have been spread out randomly all over the resort."

Mark reached for his cell. "I have to warn her."

Spencer grabbed his wrist. "You can't. She needs to act as if nothing is going on. We don't want to tip them off."

"Well, she's going to know something is up because I have to cancel our date. What exactly do you suggest I do?"

Spencer frowned then snapped his fingers. "We will use her place as cover."

"What? No way! She's freaked out enough over what's happened." Spencer was crazy if he thought he was going to involve Nicole.

"Considering she's already been a victim of these guys, I'd think she'd want to help. If they've been casing the place, they'll already know that you've been by and the two of you socialize."

"I suppose."

"Then seeing your car there again won't raise any alarm." The gleam in Spencer's eyes almost had him agreeing to the dangerous proposal—almost. "I won't put Nicole in harm's way."

"I have a plan." Spencer rubbed his chin. "But in order for it to work we'll have to let Nicole in on it."

Mark sat on the edge of the table. "This I gotta hear." One minute, Spencer refused to let Nicole know what was going on, then the next he wanted to involve her. He liked the guy, but at the moment he questioned the man's judgment.

Spencer started talking in a hushed voice. A slow, easy smile spread across Mark's face. "I'm glad *you're* wearing the wig and not me." He looked Spencer over from head to toe. "I guess you could pull off a black dress and fancy shoes, but you better hit the stores if you're going to find something in your size by tonight."

Spencer jerked his head back. "I'm not going in drag!"

"Sorry, buddy. You want to impersonate Nicole, and that's what she's wearing on our date tonight." He looked his new friend over once more and chuckled. "You could bring a female officer in on this and avoid having to shop."

Spencer turned several shades of red and stomped from the room.

Mark chuckled until he remembered he needed to fill in Nicole. He prayed she'd be willing to go along with the plan.

NICOLE SAT ON THE bed in her master bedroom listening to Mona the lead designer and her assistant Bailey discuss what needed to be done. She studied the two women. Mona, by far the older of the duo had an air of sophistication about her, but she was the consummate professional. Bailey, the polar opposite, was down to earth and reserved.

She couldn't help admire Bailey's long dark hair. Although a little frizzy, with the right treatment, the woman's hair would be like silk. Bailey took several pictures of her bedroom, then took out a tape and measured the windows and the floor space. "Do you have a color scheme in mind, Nicole?"

Nicole drew a blank. "I don't have a clue. I know it should feel peaceful and the bath should be spa-like, but beyond that I'm clueless."

Mona frowned. "How about colors you'd like to stay away from?"

"I'd say anything bold. I love white and soft grays, greens and blues."

"Good. That gives us something to work with," Mona said. "Regarding the furniture. What is your style?"

This was the part that worried Nicole the most. If she owned this place she'd go glam all the way, but this was a rental and needed to appeal to a lot of people. "Traditional?"

Mona gave her a tight smile. "Are you asking because you don't know what traditional is or you aren't sure what you like?"

Bailey caught her eye and gave her an encouraging smile. "Don't think about what anyone else would want in here. Describe to us your idea of the perfect bedroom. Trust us with the rest."

"Well, okay. Here it goes. I hate the furniture in here right now. It's too big and tired. I want light and airy, but not modern. I really like how the rest of this place has been decorated. The white leather couch is my favorite. A sparkly chandelier would be neat as well as reflective surfaces, but not too much. I love luxury, so high quality linens would be nice." She shot a look toward Mona who watched her with interest. "Maybe high quality anything would be bad in a rental." She shrugged. "Anyway, the furniture should fit the space and not overpower it. And if you are going to add a dresser, please make it functional. That one is a joke. The drawers are too tiny. I think an armoire would be ideal."

Bailey looked up from the notes she was taking. "This is exactly the kind of feedback we were hoping for. What about the bathroom?"

"It should blend with the bedroom; don't you think?"

Bailey nodded. "Anything else? Do you have a preference regarding fixtures?"

"Uh." Nicole looked to Mona.

"We can update them with something classic that fits the budget," Mona said.

Relief surged through Nicole. "Perfect. Thanks!" She stood. "Are we done then?"

Mona nodded and Bailey gathered their belongings. "I'll give you a call in a few days to go over the preliminary design," Bailey said.

"Sounds good." Nicole walked them to the door. "I look

forward to seeing what you come up with." She pulled the door open and caught her breath. "Mark! You've got to stop doing that to me."

He chuckled. "Sorry about that." He nodded toward the designers, then turned his attention to Nicole. "Do you have a minute to talk privately?"

Mona bustled past. "We were on our way out, officer."

Bailey followed silently after her boss.

"Come in." Nicole motioned Mark inside. She closed the door, turned, then led him to the living room and sat on the couch. "What's going on?"

"Something's come up."

"You need to cancel tonight?" Disappointment washed over her, but she tried to hide it.

"Not exactly." He explained the plan.

She grinned. Seeing Spencer in drag would be worth postponing their date. "Count me in. It sounds like fun." Grams would love this. She had always been up for adventure, and it didn't get more adventurous than helping a cop with a stakeout.

He chuckled. "That is not the response I expected, but thank you." They firmed up the details and he left.

Nervous energy surged through Nicole. She had to do something to keep busy until her "date" tonight. She meandered up the spiral staircase to the loft and pulled the first book her hand touched off the shelf. Grams had mentioned a good book. Would she have to go through every single title on the shelves to find the clue? She'd need to read full time all summer to accomplish that. It had to be simpler than that.

Her eyes landed on a black leather King James Bible. It looked a lot like the one Grams used to read. She ran her hand over the spine then moved to the book beside it and pulled it from the shelf. She wasn't ready to open Grams' Bible yet. The missing clue must be in one of these books. If only Grams had been more specific.

CHAPTER ELEVEN

NICOLE CLOSED THE BLINDS IN PREPARATION for the stakeout Mark and Spencer had planned. It wouldn't do to have the bad guys see cops inside her house. She stilled and stared out the window as a deer munched on weeds. The peace the animal exhibited was opposite to her own right now—she was not an adrenaline junky, and her palms sweated.

She closed the blind and moved to the next. A knock sliced through the silence squelching her thoughts. Nicole's heels tapped on the hardwood floor as she hustled to answer the door. "You're early."

"Sorry. I forgot to mention the time-line moved up."

Her stomach flipped, and her pulse thrummed in her ears. This had to be the craziest thing she'd ever agreed to, but if it helped catch the thieves, then it was worth it. "Not a problem. Let me grab my bag." She opened the newly reinforced door further, allowing him to step inside.

"You look amazing." He placed a soft kiss on her cheek and whispered, "I promise I'll make this up to you."

His touch sent a tingle racing across her skin in a way she wouldn't mind revisiting when she wasn't so nervous. She reminded herself Mark was only playing a part in case anyone was watching, or he never would have kissed her cheek since she'd made it clear they were only two friends enjoying dinner together.

Nicole turned and grabbed her bag from the counter, complete with plenty of reading material to keep her occupied all night if necessary. She'd searched through a quarter of the books in the loft for a clue, but had come up empty other than finding several that she wanted to read.

Grams probably didn't have this in mind when she said to have fun, but she had to admit she was, in spite of her nerves. It wasn't every day she got to participate in a police operation—well, maybe she wasn't an active participant, but this was close. As she walked back to where Mark waited, admiration lit his eyes. Her breath caught—that look sure wasn't for anyone else's benefit. Her cheeks warmed, and she shifted her gaze away. "Ready?"

Mark opened the door and followed her. She handed him the key to lock up, and he pocketed it—all part of the plan for later when he would return. He strolled beside her with his hand resting on the small of her back. "In case I forgot to mention it, I'm sorry about tonight. I was looking forward to our evening together." He spoke softly as he pulled the passenger door open to his car and waited for her to buckle up before closing it.

Moments later they were on Beaver Drive. Mark's hands gripped the steering wheel hard. "How're you doing?"

"Fine. Do you think they were watching?"

"Not likely. But you did a great job. Anyone would've believed we were heading out on a date."

For the first time she noted he wore a suit and tie. "You clean up nice."

He grinned and kept his eyes on the road. "Thanks. I appreciate your going along with this and being so understanding."

"Catch them. That's all I ask."

"We'll do our best, but tips don't always deliver the desired results."

She heard the warning and tucked it away. Would tonight be a total waste? "There's one part of the plan I don't understand. If the bad guys *were* watching us leave, and they see you and

Spencer go back so soon, won't they suspect something is up?"

He shrugged. "It's possible. But that's why we moved the timeline up a little. With any luck, Spencer and I will be back to your place long before anything happens."

She shuddered. "I can't believe they're planning to rob the house right next door. That's way too close for comfort!"

"Like I said, tips aren't always reliable. The stakeout may turn up nothing."

She pursed her lips—he could be right—but it also might turn up a couple of thieves. She gazed out the passenger window barely noticing the landscape of trees and shrubs.

"Nicole?"

"Hmm?"

"Tonight would be a good time to pray."

She swallowed the lump that suddenly formed and nodded. Was he worried? Should she be worried? How much danger would Mark and Spencer be in? "I imagine Spencer is thankful to have you as a partner."

He glanced her way. "He's not my partner."

"Okay." She wondered at the firmness of his tone and if it had anything to do with what had happened to his last partner.

Mark pulled into his driveway and killed the engine. After a long moment, he sighed and turned toward her. "I'm sorry for snapping, but I told myself I'd never work with a partner again. I'm only backup."

Sounded like the definition of a partner to her, but she wouldn't argue. She got out without waiting for Mark to open her door and eyed his modest rental. It was a typical Sunriver home, probably dating back to the seventies.

She followed him inside. The house had vaulted ceilings with skylights that illuminated a ceiling fan in the center of the room. All the blinds were closed. Someone moved in the dimly lit room, and Nicole jumped.

"It's only me." Spencer walked toward them.

Mark flipped on a light.

Nicole's eyes widened, and she touched her hand to her mouth, suppressing a giggle. Spencer wore a dress surprisingly similar to hers along with a blond wig. She turned to Mark. "You're abandoning me for her?"

Mark grinned and slapped Spencer on the back. "Yeah, she has a *great* personality."

Nicole held back a laugh. "Ah, don't worry. When I'm finished with your makeup and hair, any man, at least from a distance, won't care a hoot about your personality."

Spencer groaned. "Let's get this over with."

Mark chuckled. "This I've got to see." He pulled out a wooden chair from the table and sat.

Nicole studied her project. "I'll need to fix your hair if you want to be believable." She fingered the wig. "It's a good thing you're about my height and have a similar build."

Mark guffawed.

Spencer glared at them. "For the record, I'm bigger, but not enough anyone at a distance would notice." He lumbered to the kitchen counter and sat on a bar stool with his back to them.

Nicole pulled the band from her hair letting it fall past her shoulders, then carefully pulled the wig into a low ponytail. Last, she applied a light coat of makeup to his eyes and cheeks, just enough to give him a feminine look that clashed with his five o'clock shadow. "There." She stepped back and admired the effect. "Keep your head down when you go inside. Even someone with impaired vision would be able to tell you're not me if they get a look at that mug. You could've shaved."

Spencer ran his hand over his chin. "I shaved this morning."

"There's one thing to be thankful for," Mark said.

"What's that?" Spencer glared.

"Even in drag you don't look like a woman." Mark checked his watch. "I have an unopened disposable razor in the bathroom drawer. Hurry up and shave. We need to roll."

Spencer mumbled something as he left the room.

Mark turned to Nicole. "You'll be okay here?"

"I think so."

Sadie stood and stretched, then moved from her bed in the corner over to them, her tail wagging so fast it created a breeze.

"Sadie and I will be fine. You two stay safe."

"Always." He winked with a smile. As soon as Spencer joined them again, Mark motioned her behind the door so she wouldn't be seen when they left. A moment later the lock snapped into place. She checked out Mark's living room, then slipped the thriller she had yet to finish from her bag and snuggled into the worn brown leather couch facing the fireplace. Sadie laid down at her feet, resting her head on her paws.

Lord, it's been a long time, but if You're listening, please keep Mark and Spencer safe.

MARK CARRIED A CAN of soda over to the window where Spencer sat holding binoculars and peering through a slight crack. The wig and dress were now tucked away in a bag, and he'd changed into jeans and a T-shirt.

Mark loosened his tie and handed Spencer the soda. "Anything yet?"

"Nope." He set the can on the floor. "Nicole seems nice."

"She is. You fishing?"

"Yep." Spencer kept his attention focused on the house next door.

"Not taking the bait." He hoped Spencer noticed the edge in his voice. Nicole was not open for discussion. He liked her. He didn't enjoy using her like this, but at least she was safe at his place.

"Fine, but it could be a long night."

Mark sighed. He'd been on more than his share of stakeouts, and they were never fun. But being inside Nicole's house beat sitting in a car or on a park bench.

"Anything to eat around here? I'm starved."

"You didn't pack provisions? How many stakeouts have you been on anyway?"

"This is my first."

Mark tucked the information away and stood. "I keep emergency food stashed in my trunk. Be right back." He went to his car that he'd parked in the garage. The bag he kept stocked sat in the usual spot.

Nicole wasn't kidding about living in a quiet area. It made sense that the burglars would hit a neighborhood that was rarely occupied. The houses were all on the older side but well maintained, and he suspected they had the usual inventory thieves wanted.

He reached for the door that led into the kitchen and pushed it open. "Prepare your mouth for a feast of junk food. I have chips, trail mix, candy, bottled water and bottled coffee."

"Interesting emergency pack."

"Don't diss the grub. This is sacred food. Be glad I came prepared." He ripped open a bag of chips. "You want water or coffee?"

Spencer made a face. "No more soda?"

"I'll check the fridge." Mark opened the refrigerator, pulled out a can of Pepsi, and tossed it to him.

"Really? How am I supposed to open this now? It'll make a mess."

"What? You don't want to wear soda?" Chuckling, Mark walked over and handed him the last can. "You owe Nicole."

"Yeah, yeah." Spencer popped the drink open and took a long draw then turned back to the window. "Someone's coming!"

"Really?" Mark moved over to the window facing the house next door. Maybe this tip would pay off after all.

THE NEXT MORNING, SHORTLY after sunup, Mark stumbled into his home, bleary-eyed and grouchy. Sadie greeted him with a whine, clearly ready for breakfast. He set two large coffees on the counter then quickly fed her. "Brr." He looked around, trying to find the source of the cold. The place looked exactly as he'd left it, except the high desert night air had cooled it off to the temperature of an icebox. He noticed a window slightly cracked open in the kitchen and closed it. Nicole must be warm blooded.

A moan sounded from the couch. He turned and discovered Nicole cuddled in a ball on the man-sized couch. She stretched like a cat then sat up rubbing her eyes. He knew the moment she spotted him because she caught her breath, and her hand instantly shot to her tangled hair.

"Hey. How'd it go?" She sat up and tucked her feet beneath her.

He sat on the couch where her feet had been and handed her a coffee. "The only person we saw all night was a guy working on a hot tub. Looks like the intel was either bad, or they were tipped off."

Her lips turned down. "Why was someone working on a hot tub at night at a vacant house?"

"Good question, but we kept a close eye on him and no one else went in or out of the place."

Her shoulders drooped. "I really thought this would be over."

"Hey, don't give up hope. We'll get them sooner or later."

She still wore the black dress from last night, but the sandals were on the floor beside her. "Thanks." She took a sip and shivered.

"You cold?"

"Yeah." Her soft voice sounded like dinner music after listening to Spencer's rough bass all night.

Though tempted to scoot close and pull her into his arms to warm her, he chose the safer route and stood. "Be right back." He made a right around the corner to the hall where the linens were stored and pulled out a soft black and white checked blanket. When he came back into the room, she was running her fingers through her hair.

She spotted him watching and stopped midway down and put her hands in her lap.

"Your hair is fine." Mark wrapped a blanket around Nicole's shoulders.

Pink tinged her cheeks, and she ducked her head a little. "Thanks." She cradled the warm cup between her hands.

He motioned to the coffee. "I don't know how you like it so I grabbed a handful of stuff." He pulled French vanilla and plain creamer cups, along with packets of sugar and artificial sweeteners from his pocket, and placed them on the oversized ottoman that matched the couch.

"That was nice of you. This is perfect. When I make coffee I use French vanilla creamer."

Her pleased look made him glad he'd stopped for the brew. He took a long draw from his cup and rested his head against the couch cushions. He'd hoped the stakeout would have turned out differently, but right now all he wanted to do was sleep.

"Tell me about last night."

"Spencer talked my ear off, and I have a pounding headache."

She cringed. "Sorry about the headache. I'll get out of your hair." She moved to stand.

He stopped her with a wave of his hand. "No. Stay and drink your coffee. I have to work in an hour. I'll run you home on my way if that's all right."

"How are you supposed to stay up all night and ride all

day?"

"Didn't you know cops are like doctors? We can go for days without sleep." He yawned. "But I admit it was easier when I was in my twenties."

She chuckled. "How old are you anyway?"

"Thirty-two."

"You're an *old* man!"

The lightness in her voice made him smile. "And how old are you?"

She shook her head. "Didn't anyone ever teach you not to ask a woman her age?"

"Sure, but you're just a kid." He kept a straight face. "So it doesn't count."

She reached behind her back, grabbed the pillow then tossed it at his head.

He easily dodged it. "See what I mean?" He raised a brow.

Nicole smirked. "I'm twenty-eight."

"I'm only four years older than you. Guess you better enjoy your youth while it lasts. You'll be an old woman before you know it." He winked and stood. "I'm going to clean up, then I'll run you home."

"That works. You hungry? I could whip up scrambled eggs—if you have any eggs."

"Perfect. While you're at it, will you let Sadie out?"

"Sure."

He drained the last of his coffee and tossed the cup in the kitchen trash before heading to his bedroom. He looked in the mirror and realized he was still smiling. The woman was full of surprises. Before he brought her over last night, he'd Googled her and discovered she didn't do the whole social networking thing, but he was able to determine she graduated with honors from Oregon State University. She had a clean record too, not even a parking ticket. Surprising considering how many times he could have ticketed her since they'd met.

He yawned. They'd better solve this case soon or he'd be falling asleep on the job, and that couldn't happen. Maybe he should run Nicole home then call in sick. No. If Spencer could work, so could he. He yawned again—this was going to be a long day. He prayed it'd be uneventful.

CHAPTER TWELVE

NICOLE SAT AT HER KITCHEN TABLE beside Bailey who explained her design proposal, her enthusiasm contagious. "I really like the bedframe. I never would have thought I'd like that bold of a design, but the white color lightens it up."

"Exactly. And we will add pops of color with the accessories. That makes the furniture very versatile."

"What about the wall color?" Nicole couldn't believe how much she was getting into this, considering it wasn't even her home, but she'd caught Bailey's passion for designing and couldn't help getting excited about the final product.

"I brought samples with me." She pulled a color-wheel style paint sample from her bag.

"Uh, that's more than a few."

Bailey laughed. "We are only looking at these." She manipulated the wheel to show two strips of colors.

"Oh. Is that a gray or blue?"

Bailey held the sample up to the light. "Gray-blue. Is that the one you like best?"

"I think so. What about you?"

"I like it. We can add sparkle with the chandelier." She pressed a button and pulled up pictures of lighting.

Nicole grinned. "I should have become a designer. This is fun." She pointed to her favorites. They continued like this for the next hour, with Bailey showing her samples and Nicole noting her favorites.

Bailey closed her laptop. "Well, that does it. I'll order

everything we need. My crew will be here next week to haul out the old stuff. Make sure you get all your personal belongings moved into the guest room before Monday morning. They will be here bright and early to get started."

"How long will it take?"

"I need to talk budget with Mona. It really depends on how extensive a remodel we do in the bathroom. It could take a few days if we only do cosmetic stuff to a couple of weeks if we start ripping things out and find hidden issues like dry rot."

"Good to know." She pushed back and stood. "I suppose you get this kind of job all the time."

Bailey raised a manicured brow. "If you mean makeovers, yes. But if you mean a situation like yours, this is a first for me." Her eyes sparkled as she smiled.

"I'm here for the summer and don't know a lot of people. Maybe we could have coffee sometime. I kind of get sick of myself." Nicole chuckled.

"That sounds like fun. Mona keeps me on a pretty tight leash, but if we call it a design meeting and mix business with pleasure, I think that would be very doable. In fact," she pulled out her phone and pressed the screen. "How about we plan to meet on Friday morning at nine. I'll know the scope of the project by then, and you can give final approval on the project details."

"Perfect. Where do you want to meet? I've only been to the Merchant Trader at the lodge."

"That works for me. I'll see you then." Bailey saw herself out.

Nicole slid on flip-flops and strolled out to her deck. Warmth wrapped its soothing arms around her, and the smell of pine tickled her nose. She sneezed. Maybe sitting outside wasn't the best idea considering her allergies, but she refused to be confined indoors.

She loved listening to the sound of children laughing and people talking as they rode or strolled past on the nearby bike path. What she really enjoyed, though, was hanging out poolside.

And Sarah had asked her to check up on Connor at the North pool. She'd bring a book and soak up some rays, but this time she'd be sure to apply sunblock first. It was nice that anyone staying in Sunriver could use the swimming pool as long as they had a pass or paid a fee to get in.

She quickly readied herself then drove to the North swimming pool. Her flip-flops smacked against her heels as she walked across the street.

She spotted Connor lounging by the pool and stopped at the fence. "Hey, Connor!" She waved to get his attention.

He waved back and jogged across the grass to her. "What's up?"

"Not much."

"You going to come in and swim, or read?" He pointed to her bag with a book sticking out the top. A knowing look lit his eyes.

"I thought I might take a dip to cool off and then read. Are you here with friends?"

He nodded and pointed to a couple of boys competing to see whose cannonball made the biggest splash. "Yeah. Sit far away from them if you don't want to get wet."

"Good advice. Thanks." She strolled to the office and handed her pass to the attendant. A minute later she pulled a lounge chair out of the splash zone and settled in for a good read.

Shouting drew her from her book. She looked in the direction of the commotion, jumped up and darted over to where Connor and another boy were throwing punches. "Hey! Knock it off!" She stepped between the kids and received a fist in the gut courtesy of the other kid. She doubled over.

"Enough!" A lifeguard glowered over them. "You boys are banned from the pool." He looked at Nicole, concern in his eyes. "Are you okay?"

"I'll live."

"Thanks for intervening."

Connor strode toward the exit.

"Excuse me." Nicole tossed the words at the lifeguard then rushed to the lounge chair. She swept up her belongings then darted after Connor. "Wait up!"

He didn't slow.

She ran and caught up to him on the other side of the fence. "Connor, stop!"

He stood still, breathing hard, fists clenched at his sides.

"What happened back there?"

"I don't want to talk about it."

"Too bad. You can either tell me, or I can call your cousin."

"No!" Panic shone in his eyes. "Please, Nicole. It's not a big deal."

"I disagree. If you don't want to tell me what happened, then maybe you'd rather talk with Mark."

Connor toed a pebble. "Yeah, I think I would."

"Fine." She pulled out her cell phone and sent him a text. A moment later he replied to meet him at the police department. "Come on. I'll drive." She walked toward her car, which was parked across the street. "Hop in." A few minutes later she texted Mark to let him know they were waiting outside the PD for him.

Dressed in uniform, Mark pushed out the door and smiled when he spotted them. "How are two of my favorite people?"

"We've been better." She quickly explained what went down at the pool then walked away. If Connor didn't want to share with her then that was fine. At least he was willing to talk with Mark. She found a bench to sit on about a hundred feet away. What had set the kids off? She rubbed her stomach. At least the boy didn't deliver too much of a wallop, but her midriff would probably be sore tomorrow. Her knee bounced up and down at a rapid pace. When she'd come to Sunriver she hadn't anticipated becoming a part of so many lives. She had more of a life in Sunriver than at home.

Could God be trying to tell her something? Maybe He

wanted her to move here. She shook her head—impossible. The homes were out of her reach, and she had no job. No. Come the end of August, she'd head home to Corvallis unless something came of her application to the local school. Her stomach knotted at the thought of returning home without a job—or was it returning home and leaving Sunriver and all the friends she'd made here that really bothered her?

Mark and Connor approached. Mark's serious face put her nerves on edge. She stood. He leaned toward her and whispered. "I'll call you later." Then he turned to the boy. "Don't forget what we talked about."

"I won't."

"Good. I'll stop by your place on my route later."

"You don't have to." The boy kept his head down.

He rested a hand on Connor's shoulder. "I want to."

Connor squinted at him. "Okay."

"I'll give you a ride home." Nicole pulled car keys from her purse and mouthed thank you to Mark. The man had a huge heart. It seemed he made a habit of going above and beyond for everyone in his life.

He nodded and waved.

Nicole was accustomed to dealing with the occasional altercation in the classroom and on the playground, but this was different somehow. Connor walked silently beside her and slid into the car without a word. Had she ruined their friendship today? She'd only wanted to help.

With a sigh, she started the car and headed to Sarah's. At least her friend would be home in a couple of hours and Mark would be stopping in, so Connor wouldn't be alone for long. A couple of minutes later, she pulled onto Sarah's street and stopped in front of her house. "Are you angry with me?"

"No. Just embarrassed. I'm sorry about what happened earlier. I hope you're not hurt."

A smile touched her lips and she breathed easy for the first time since the incident at the pool. "I'll live. If you need anything—"

"I won't, but thanks." He hopped out and rushed inside.

She pulled away from the house and drove home. Mark's call couldn't come soon enough. Curiosity ate at her.

SEVERAL HOURS AFTER MEETING with Connor and Nicole, Mark pulled to a stop in front of Nicole's place. He'd promised to call but would rather talk in person. Connor said she'd taken a punch to the gut. The front door opened, and Nicole stood there with a perplexed look.

"This is a surprise. Come in."

He followed her inside then out onto the deck.

"I've been waiting for you to call for the past three hours."

"Sorry. My shift just ended." He sat in one of the teak chairs, and the other chair creaked as she settled in the one next to him. "I heard you were injured today."

"I'm fine. Had the wind knocked out of me for a moment, but that was all."

"You could press charges."

"Oh, I don't think that's necessary. Do you?"

"Not really, but I wanted you to know." Mark rested his forearms on his knees and stared at the deck under his feet, buying himself some time. How much should he tell her? He leaned back in the chair. "Connor was defending you."

"What?" Alarm replaced the concern. "What do you mean he was defending me? I was minding my own business and reading a book nowhere near the kids."

He shook his head. "Not what I meant. The other boy made a rude remark about you so Connor took a swing at him."

"Oh. I had no idea. Why would he do that?"

100

"It's a guy thing."

"That's nuts. What did he say?"

"It's not important. What is important is that Connor felt very bad about everything, including choosing to hit the kid. I talked to him, and I think he understands that in the future there are better ways of handling situations like that."

Nicole's distressed look made him chuckle. "What's wrong?"

"I can't believe he got in a fight because of me. I feel awful. I was only trying to help Sarah, and I ended up making a mess of things."

He reached for her hand and ran his thumb across the top. "It wasn't your fault. Let it go." He gently squeezed her hand then stood up. "I should head home. It's been a long day." A frustrating day to be exact. They were no closer to solving the burglaries, and two more houses had been hit while he was off duty.

Nicole stood and faced him. "Okay. Thanks for helping with Connor and for stopping by." She walked him to the door. "If you weren't in a rush, I'd offer you dinner."

He hesitated. Was she still feeling uncomfortable being here alone? "I could eat."

She laughed, slipped her fingers around his forearm, and tugged him into the kitchen before moving to the fridge. He missed her touch. He cleared his throat, unwilling to follow the direction his thoughts were taking. "What are we eating?" In truth, she could've been serving sand, and he wouldn't have noticed. What was happening to him? He enjoyed being with Nicole way too much.

"You look deep in thought. Care to share, or is it work related?"

He shook his head. "My thoughts are best left up here." He tapped his head. If she had an inkling of what he was thinking she would probably bolt. Yes, he definitely needed to keep his thoughts to himself.

CHAPTER THIRTEEN

NICOLE PAID FOR A LARGE MOCHA at the Merchant Trader Café then walked outside onto the deck. Bailey called saying she was running late. Considering Nicole had nothing on her schedule for the day, Bailey's tardiness didn't matter.

She sipped the drink slowly, hoping it would last until the designer arrived. Beyond the deck, golf carts rolled past. A couple of kids and their parents were on the putting green. Maybe she'd try it out before the end of summer.

A commotion near the door that led inside drew her attention. Her eyes widened. Bailey crouched to pick up a messenger bag. Grams would have called it a fancy briefcase. At least she hadn't dropped her drink. She stood, blew her bangs out of her eyes, then waved when she spotted Nicole.

Nicole pushed a chair out for her. "Rough morning?"

"Aren't all mornings rough?" Bailey sat.

Nicole shook her head. "I love mornings. It's the best time of the day."

Bailey chuckled. "If you say so. Clearly I'm not a morning person." She opened her messenger bag and pulled out a tablet. "Good thing I didn't have my laptop in here. At least I have a protective case around my tablet." She powered on the device and adjusted it so they could see the images better. "I'm glad you sat in the shade or we wouldn't be able to see the screen." She pulled up an image and handed over the device. "What do you think?" Anxiety filled her face.

Nicole stared at the screen. Her room was beautiful, and the bathroom though small, looked spa-like with white quartz counters mounted on a new vanity, a new tiled shower and tile flooring. "I love it. The budget was big enough to do *all* of this?"

"Yes. If you give your approval, work will begin on Monday morning. I will be there to get things started, but then the contractors will take over. Once the big work is completed, I'll do the finishing touches. The project will take a full week to complete, possibly longer depending on what we find once we pull everything out. To be safe plan on two weeks."

Under promise over deliver. She hoped it really could get done that fast, but Bailey seemed confident. Nicole couldn't stop smiling. "I feel like I have a fairy godmother. Then again, this isn't my house." She sipped her now lukewarm mocha.

"Would you do anything differently if it were your place?"

Would she? "No. I don't think so. I love all the choices right down to the flooring."

"Then we accomplished our goal." Bailey's face lit when she smiled.

Though the designer's features were plain, and her bangs hung too low, the more she got to know Bailey, the more she realized there was a beautiful woman hiding behind large glasses, and too much hair around her face. Not that it mattered. Bailey was a sweetheart, but Nicole couldn't help but wonder why a woman with her design sense would try to be invisible. At least that's the way it appeared to her.

"So what do you do for fun around here?" Nicole asked.

"If you like the outdoors then you are in the perfect place. What kinds of things do you enjoy?"

"I've enjoyed tennis, bicycling and hanging out by the pool, but I know there must be more than that around here."

"Oh yeah." Bailey named a litany of activities. "Personally I like the winter sports, although I'm not good at them. The last time I went ice-skating it was a disaster. And forget about skiing. But Bachelor has inner tubing, which brings out the kid in me." A smile lit her face.

"Me too! There's a hill near my house, and if we get enough snow I'm right there with all the kids. But skiing is my favorite."

"Not me. I'll stick to inner tubing, thank you very much. The idea of barreling down the side of a mountain on two tiny skis is more adventure than this girl can handle." Bailey laughed as she tucked the tablet back into her bag. "I should head out. Mona will wonder what happened to me if I'm gone too long." She stood.

"I'll walk out with you." Nicole stood and tossed her cup in the trash. "Do you like your boss?"

"Mona is a fantastic designer, and I'm honored to work for her. I've learned a lot."

Nicole noted she didn't really answer the question, but it wasn't a fair question, so she dropped it. They strolled through the café and the connecting store then left the building coming out by the stone waterfall Nicole had admired her first day here.

Nicole waved. "See you Monday." With a little extra bounce in her step, she headed to her car. Grams would be tickled. Not only had she gone an entire morning without stressing her job situation, she'd had fun, and she hoped, made a new friend.

A kid flew by on his bike. She did a double take—Connor. The boy really needed to follow the rules before he hurt himself or someone else. Tires squealed. She turned toward the sound. *Connor!* Her heart rate kicked into double time.

She sprinted to the boy who lay on the pavement, and dropped to her knees beside him. He groaned and held his arm. "Where are you hurt?"

"My arm."

The male driver stood beside the hood of the car presumably calling 911.

"Do you hurt anyplace else?"

"No." Connor sat up. "I think I'm okay. That was so stupid."

"Agreed. You need to be more careful. You're lucky you weren't seriously hurt. Can you stand?"

Sirens sounded nearby, and a moment later a police cruiser came into view.

Connor groaned. "Why are the cops here?" He stood and sucked in a breath. "That stings."

"What?"

He pointed to his scraped and bloodied knee.

Spencer bolted from the cruiser and approached. "Hi, Nicole. Did you hit this kid?"

"No officer. I did." The man looked nervous and angry. "He whipped around the corner and darted right in front of me. I slammed on my brakes but couldn't stop fast enough."

Nicole noticed the man's cracked windshield and cringed. She turned to Connor. "Good thing you were wearing a helmet." From the look of the windshield Connor was fortunate he wasn't seriously injured.

An ambulance pulled to a stop nearby and two medics approached.

"I'm okay," Connor said, but his face registered pain.

Nicole placed a gentle hand on his shoulder. "Connor, Spencer is a friend of Mark's. I think he'd want you to do what these people say."

"Who's going to take care of my car?" The man who hit him crossed his arms and glowered down at them.

Spencer stood and moved the man away from them. The medics took Connor over to the ambulance.

Nicole pulled out her cell and called Sarah. She explained what happened.

"Is he okay?" Panic filled Sarah's voice.

"I think so. Nothing looks broken from what I can see, but the medics are with him now. I'll let you talk to one of them." She walked over and explained she had Connor's guardian on the phone and handed it over to the woman.

The EMT finished bandaging Connor's knee. "You're a lucky boy."

"How's his arm?" Nicole asked.

"It's hard to say for sure without an x-ray, but it doesn't appear to be broken."

The woman handed Nicole the cell phone back. "I'm here, Sarah."

"I'm leaving the office now. Please take Connor home for me. I told the medic that I don't want them to take him to the hospital. You'll need to sign the waiver for me. I'll meet you at my place." She tucked her phone into her pocket and pivoted to the boy. "You ready to go? I'm taking you home." She quickly signed the wavier.

"What about my bike?"

Spencer cleared his throat.

Nicole looked over her shoulder. "I didn't realize you were there, Spencer."

He nodded. "I took the driver's statement. Did you see what happened?"

Nicole told him what she saw before the accident and what she'd heard. "I need to take Connor home now. Can we go?"

"What about my bike?" Connor asked again.

"I'll bring it to your house," Spencer said. "Although it's a little banged up."

Connor sighed. "I want to go home now," his voice wobbled.

Nicole immediately strode to her car, expecting he'd follow. She unlocked the car and slid behind the wheel. Connor got into the passenger seat. They drove in silence to Sarah's house. When she parked, he bolted and went inside, slamming the door behind him.

"I guess I'll wait out here." She put the windows down and got out a few minutes later when Spencer pulled up.

"How's he doing?"

"I think he's more upset about his bike than anything. That's how he gets around. It will be a long summer without wheels."

Spencer frowned. "He should have thought of that before

riding recklessly."

She nodded. "His cousin will be here soon. Maybe you could leave his bike by the door."

"I need to talk with her before I leave."

"Oh." She wished Mark was here. She leaned against her car. "How's the burglary case coming?"

"Still open."

She nodded. "I hope you catch them soon."

"That's the plan." He checked his watch.

She couldn't blame him for being short. He was probably anxious to get back to his case.

Sarah finally pulled up beside her car. She flung the door open. "Where's Connor?"

Spencer stepped forward. "He's inside. We need to talk."

"Okay." Sarah gave Nicole a quick hug. "Thank you for being there and contacting me."

"Of course. Call me later."

Sarah nodded before turning and going inside with Spencer.

Nicole blew out a breath. What a way to start the day. Poor Connor and Sarah. Hopefully everything would turn out okay.

MONDAY MORNING NICOLE SAT outside on her deck with a cup of coffee and a book. She'd all but given up on Grams' game. If she didn't find the book Grams' was talking about soon, she didn't know what she'd do.

She tried to tune out the racket going on inside as the men demoed the master bathroom, but every time they tossed something into the garbage bin out front she startled.

"Hello!" A woman called.

Nicole stood. "Bailey?" She strolled to the gate and looked over the top. "Hey there. I wasn't sure when you'd be here. I'm hanging out here."

"I don't blame you. Let me check on the guys then I'll join you."

Nicole sneezed. Hopefully her allergies wouldn't give her too much trouble, or she'd be forced to retreat indoors. She sneezed again and rubbed her itchy eyes. Maybe reading in the loft would be a better idea, but she'd wait to meet with Bailey first.

A short time later Bailey strolled onto the deck. "Things are moving right along and the good news is everything looks as it should. No bad pipes or rotten wood."

"Great! Do you have time to join me for a glass of lemonade?" She stood. "I made some fresh squeezed this morning."

"Yum. I can't say no to that. Thanks."

"Have a seat. I'll be right back." She went inside and quickly filled two glasses. The sound of hammering made her wince. She rushed back onto the deck. "Here you go. I hope you like it. My Grandmother used to make this all the time."

Bailey sipped the beverage. "It's perfect." She set the glass on the patio table. "I hope the remodel doesn't become too much of a burden for you."

Nicole waved a hand. "It's fine."

"If you say so. I wouldn't want to listen to that racket all day." She took another sip. "But the end result will be worth all the headaches. My favorite part is yet to come."

Nicole leaned forward. "What would that be?"

"When all the finishing touches are put into place and you see if for the first time. Please promise me you won't peek. It will spoil all my fun."

Nicole chuckled. "Sure. I promise." She never dreamed such a request would be made, but there was really no reason for her to go into the master suite. She'd moved into the other bedroom containing a second full bath, so obliging Bailey would be no trouble.

"Thanks. I knew I liked you from the moment we met."

Nicole's phone rang. She didn't recognize the number, and considered ignoring it, but curiosity got the best of her. "Excuse me for a minute."

"I should be going anyway. I'll be in touch." Bailey stood and exited through the gate.

"Hello. This is Nicole."

"Hey there. How's it going?"

"Mark?" He must be using someone else's phone.

"I can't reach Connor. He left me a cryptic message and asked me to call him. Do you have any idea what he's up to?"

Nicole frowned. "Sorry, no. I've been at my place all day."

"Okay. I'll swing by Sarah's and check on him. That boy attracts trouble like a dog to a flea."

She chuckled. "Okay. Let me know if you need anything, but he is probably lonely and wants company." She said goodbye and set the phone beside her. Hopefully not being able to reach Connor wasn't a sign of trouble, and he was only seeking companionship.

CHAPTER FOURTEEN

A WEEK LATER, NICOLE RAN HARD for the tennis ball, took a swing, and missed. Sarah was good—way out of Nicole's league. Down by five points and it was her serve. Tossing the ball above her head, Nicole raised her arm and whipped it forward, sending the ball slightly past the centerline in the right corner.

Sarah drilled the ball just out of Nicole's reach.

Nicole chased after the ball then pocketed it. Wiping sweat from her face, she laughed. "I haven't been beaten that badly in a long time."

"Give yourself some credit. You're not accustomed to playing someone who spends a couple hours a day working on her game."

Nicole's eyes widened. "Are you serious? How do you have that much time when you work all day? No wonder I'm getting creamed. You're practically a professional with all that court time." She followed her friend, and they strolled toward the parking lot beside the basketball court where Connor was working on his free-throw.

Sarah laughed. "Not even close, but thanks. Most evenings after work I head down here with Connor and a few of my friends join me for a game. It's nice to have someone new to challenge me."

"Ha. My skills aren't much of a challenge. You were holding out on me the last time we played."

A grin spread across Sarah's face. "True."

Nicole nudged her playfully. "What exactly do you do for a

living?"

"Mortgage broker. I really enjoy my job. It's fun helping people get into a home."

"Maybe I should look into doing that. This area seems to have a hot real estate market."

"I thought you were a school teacher."

"I am, at least I was, but it's time to consider other options since I haven't been able to find a position for this coming school year." She loved teaching, but she also enjoyed paying her bills in full and on time, which wouldn't happen if she didn't find a job soon.

"Don't give up, Nicole. Something is bound to turn up." Sarah put her racket and ball bag into the trunk of her car. "Want to take a cool down walk around the park?"

"Sure. Mind if I dump my stuff first?" She motioned toward her car.

"Go ahead. I'll walk with you."

"How is Connor doing? I haven't seen him at all the past several days." Granted she'd been spending a lot of time at her house, but she usually ran into the boy when she went into the village.

Sarah waved a hand. "He's incredibly resilient and healing fast. Without wheels he hasn't ventured far from my place." She lowered her voice as she glanced toward the basketball court. "But he told me he's embarrassed that you keep seeing him make a fool of himself. I think he might have a little crush on you."

"Oh no."

Her friend nodded. "Don't worry. These things pass. I once had a crush on one of my teachers, so I'm speaking from experience. I'm sure he'll be back to himself in no time."

"I hope you're right." She waggled her eyebrows. "You crushed on your teacher?"

Sarah rolled her eyes. "All the girls in my seventh grade glass had a crush on Mr. Price, but I got over it after he gave me an F."

Nicole laughed. "I'm sorry for laughing, but that does not sound like you at all."

"Good. I'd hate to think my adult self resembles who I was at twelve."

Nicole sobered. "Back to Connor. I feel badly about what happened at the pool."

"Stop. You only went there because I asked you to—which by the way, I told Connor. He had it in his head . . . well, never mind, but all is well. So relax."

Nicole worried her bottom lip. "Okay, I'll try."

"You should come to my church on Sunday. We're having a community potluck. I'm bringing my famous pudding salad. It's so yummy—whipped topping, vanilla pudding, and fruit."

"Healthy and decadent. Sounds delicious. Count me in." Nicole tilted her head. "I didn't realize you go to church."

"I've been attending the community church ever since I moved here."

Nicole pulled her keys from her bag. She'd been giving her relationship with the Lord a lot of thought. Getting back into church would be good, and Grams would definitely approve. "It won't bother Connor to see me there?"

"I don't think so."

"Good. What should I bring?"

"If you don't cook, I suggest something easy. How about chips or a pasta salad from a deli?"

Nicole tossed her stuff in the trunk. "I never said I couldn't cook. Maybe I'll bring brownies."

"Great idea. There's never enough dessert at these things." The twinkle in her friend's eyes belied the truth of her words. They marched back to the trail to walk until Connor was ready to leave.

"I don't care. Dessert is *my* specialty." Nicole watched a couple of boys playing catch on the ball field near the basketball court. Seeing all the kids here in Sunriver made her miss her students. No, she wouldn't go there. They walked past the outfield and headed away from the tennis courts.

"Have you run into Mark lately?"

"Why do you ask?" Nicole shot her friend a sideways glance.

"No reason really. I thought I saw something between you, that's all, and according to Connor the two of you are friendly."

"Well," she drew the word out.

"You *have* seen him!" Sarah grabbed her arm, pulling her to a stop. "Tell me what happened." She sounded like a kid at Christmas.

Nicole shrugged, trying to keep her expression neutral. "There's not much to tell really. We've run into each other several times, and he responded to the break-in at my house."

"The what? You mean someone broke into your place?"

"Yes. A couple of weeks ago. It was pretty awful, but they didn't take much really. I walked in before they were finished and got whacked on the back of my head."

"No way! That's horrible."

"I'm surprised Connor didn't tell you."

"He knew?"

Nicole cringed at the volume of Sarah's voice. "I was upset, but it's not a big deal anymore. Mark told me some things I could do to make the place safer, and I feel much better now."

"I don't know about things where you come from, but any kind of break-in around here is a big deal. It doesn't happen in Sunriver. I was talking to my friends Tina and Marge about that very thing before they left. They'd heard that homes were being robbed and were concerned for me. I told them they'd heard wrong, but I guess I'm the one who was wrong."

"Where are your friends from anyway?"

"Bend. They were on a staycation."

"Seriously? That's only a short drive from here."

"I know." She stepped around a rock. "The girls actually popped in again one evening last week after spending a couple of

114

weeks crashing in my guest room. I was sure surprised to see them again so soon."

Nicole shrugged. She didn't want to say anything rude about Sarah's friends so she kept quiet. They seemed so rough around the edges compared to Sarah, that it amazed her Sarah hung out with them. "How did you and your friends meet?"

Sarah frowned and started walking again. "We go way back to my B.C. days."

"You lost me."

"Sorry. Before Christ. You know, before I got into church and became a Christian. It's been kind of tough maintaining our friendship because those two don't want anything to do with the Lord, and they give me a hard time about my faith. In answer to your question, we met at a party years ago."

"Sounds like you don't have much in common with them anymore."

"I suppose. We still enjoy getting together every now and then, but only for short periods of time. Honestly this last visit was a little too long for my liking."

Nicole stayed by her side as they finished the loop and ended in the parking lot beside Sarah's car. "So next week, same time and place?"

"Yep, but I'll see you at church on Sunday, right?"

Nicole nodded and felt like an airhead. She'd already forgotten about the potluck.

Sarah pulled open the car door and reached inside. "This flyer has all the details."

Nicole took the paper regarding the church potluck. She gave it a quick glance and tucked it into her purse. "Thanks. See you Sunday."

CHAPTER FIFTEEN

MARK STOOD IN THE BUFFET LINE at Community Bible Church. He honed in on a platter of crispy fried chicken. Something about a potluck made fried chicken taste even better than usual. Piling his plate high with an assortment of fruit, pasta, salads, and chicken, he turned from the table and collided with Connor, very nearly dropping the masterpiece he held.

He tousled the kid's hair. "Whoa, sorry about that. How's the arm?"

"Better, but still sore." Connor nodded toward Mark's plate. "That looks good."

"I'm glad your arm's improving."

"Me too. Sarah's taking me to buy a new bike this afternoon. I can't wait."

It didn't surprise him that the boy missed his wheels. "You'd better get in line before the food is gone."

"Sarah's holding my spot." He turned to face the front of the line. "Oh, she's almost to the food. Gotta go, 'bye."

Mark chuckled and pivoted toward a set of chairs lined up against a wall, but stopped as his gaze landed on a familiar face. Nicole stood in the doorway. His stomach lurched. He walked up to her. "Hey there. You should've told me you were coming."

"Sarah invited me." She pointed toward the line where her friend stood. "I didn't realize this was your church, too."

"I'm really glad you came." He motioned with his plate toward the buffet table. "Join me when you have your food?"

A pensive look covered her face as she glanced around the

room.

"Relax. The people here are nice."

"That's a relief. I was pretty nervous about coming." She eyed his plate. "Maybe you could share some of yours. There appears to be enough for us both." Her eyes twinkled with mischief.

He pulled the plate closer. "No pillaging my feast. Get your own." He pointed to the line. "I'll save you a seat."

She flipped her hair over her shoulder. "I'll remember this act of greed, and someday when you're starving and about ready to faint from lack of food, you'll regret not sharing."

Mark chuckled. He liked this playful side of Nicole very much. He watched as she scooted into the dwindling line. He spooned a bite of pasta salad into his mouth and nearly gagged on the strong taste of garlic. That was a mistake. He swallowed hard and washed it down with water. People meandered by with their plates, and a few children darted between them. It'd be a feat if they all made it to seats without spilling.

Connor plunked down beside him and wolfed his food. "See you later."

"Nice talking to you." How the boy managed to eat a plateful in less than two minutes escaped him.

He looked sheepish. "Sorry. I can't talk and eat."

"I guess it's safer that way."

"Huh?"

"Less chance of choking."

Connor chuckled. "Right. See you." He waved and slipped into the throng of people milling about.

Mark bit into the chicken.

"How is it?"

He looked up into Nicole's emerald green eyes. "Cold but delicious."

She sat in the folding chair beside him. "Good. I'm glad I grabbed a piece."

He noted her selection of food and was impressed by the healthful choices—fresh fruit, green salad with a vinaigrette dressing, a whole-wheat roll and one piece of chicken. "You're missing a major food group."

"Huh?" She studied her plate.

"Dessert."

She nudged him in the shoulder. "I try and skip that food group as often as possible."

"Bor-ing."

He broke his brownie in half and placed it on her plate. "You can't sit by me and not indulge a little." He lowered his voice and leaned close. "I heard one of the other men say these were the best brownies he'd ever tasted."

NICOLE BEAMED A SMILE toward Mark. Knowing that the church people enjoyed her baking made her all the more happy she'd decided to come to the potluck. She'd popped in before the service ended to drop off her contribution to the meal then waited for Sarah. "I baked those brownies. It's my grandma's recipe."

"You made the brownies? And you don't eat dessert?"

She nodded.

He took a bite. "They're really good."

"Thanks."

"What are your plans for the rest of the day? I'd love to take a few brownies to work tomorrow. I'd be willing to help bake." He tilted his head to the side.

Nicole stuffed a large bite of salad into her mouth and chewed slowly. She'd had a lot of downtime lately, which meant an abundance of time to think. She liked Mark and enjoyed being with him, but she could see the direction their friendship was taking, and it made her uneasy. His profession wasn't exactly safe.

Did she really want to pursue anything more than friendship? The more time she spent with him, the more she worried. "How about I make up a couple batches and drop them by the station sometime this week?"

"Really? That'd be great. Thanks!" Mark took the last bite of chicken and grinned as he set his plate aside. Holding a napkin, he touched it to the tip of her mouth. "You had a little dressing."

A tingle zipped from her toes to her fingers. "Uh, thanks."

"If you're not busy, we could go do something else today. The weather is perfect for being outdoors." He quirked his head to the side, his eyes vulnerable.

She blinked rapidly. How could he look so adorable, vulnerable, and strong at the same time? She wanted to say yes. But what about keeping her distance and sticking to friendship? Granted being outdoors would be much less confining than baking in her small kitchen.

"Come on, Nicole. I can tell you want to."

"May I be honest?"

"Of course."

"I like you, Mark, but you're a cop and that makes me nervous."

"I'm a regular guy who wants to spend an afternoon with the prettiest girl in the room. Forget about my occupation."

Her cheeks burned as she studied his face. "Okay."

He pumped a fist in the air.

Laughter bubbled up from deep inside her. Once she gained control, she sobered. "What did you have in mind?"

"Do you hike? We could hike to Benham Falls."

Hiking wasn't her favorite activity. She much preferred tennis or water sports or something that didn't involve climbing over dusty trails and risking an encounter with a snake. She pursed her lips then snapped her fingers. "Are you interested in helping fulfill a girl's dream?"

He quirked a brow.

"The house where I'm staying has a tandem bike, and I've always wanted to try riding one."

He made a face.

She quickly added. "It's okay to say no. I could ask Sarah sometime. I know you spend a ton of time on a bike seat."

He groaned, then flashed a crooked smile. "I suppose there are worse ways to spend a Sunday afternoon. But . . ."

Nicole could tell by the twinkle in his eyes he was going to say yes. She stood to toss her garbage. "You ready?"

"Now?"

She looked around the emptying room. "Why not?" If they didn't get a move on, she'd talk herself out of spending the afternoon with him. "Let me say goodbye to Sarah. Be right back." When she'd told her friend about Mark's request she sit with him, Sarah encouraged Nicole to join him. If she didn't know better, she'd think Grams had planted Mark in her life. Grams might be able to pull off a scavenger hunt of sorts, but there was no way she'd arranged for Nicole to meet the man of her dreams.

Her brain stuttered. Impossible—Mark couldn't be the man of her dreams. He lived in the biggest city in Oregon and had a dangerous job. She didn't like big cities, and she definitely didn't like danger. Especially where people she cared about were concerned.

NICOLE WHEELED THE TANDEM from her garage. "Here it is. What do you think?" Her nose tickled and she held back a sneeze.

Mark pushed on the tires and gave the bike a general once over. "Looks sound. The tires are a little low, but we can fill them at the North gas station."

"Okay. You want the front or back? On second thought, you take the front." She didn't want him staring at her backside—not that he would since he was a gentleman, but still . . .

He straddled the bike. "Can you believe I've never ridden one of these things?"

"Me neither." She pulled the garage door closed then got on behind him. She scrunched her nose trying to hold in a sneeze. Her eyes watered. She would not sneeze. "*Ah-choo!*"

"Catching a cold?"

"Allergies. They're usually mild, but they've been bothering me for several days, even with allergy meds." Another sneeze escaped.

"Sorry to hear that. You sure you want to go riding?" He looked over his shoulder.

"Positive." Then again, maybe this wasn't such a good idea. They were both inexperienced on a tandem bike, and she didn't want to break a limb. Plus, her head was beginning to ache from the congestion that had suddenly attacked her.

He pushed off and pedaled. Too late to back out now. Besides the alternative was hanging out inside the close quarters of her house. She copied his motion and within seconds they bumped through the dirt to the path.

After pedaling for a while, she realized Mark could do all the work, and she could coast along. Good thing too because she'd started to wheeze. Odd. Her asthma almost never acted up. It hadn't been much of a problem for years. She tried to ignore the wheezing and relax. There was no reason to push her body if it wasn't necessary.

Mark grunted. "Think you could help pedal up the hill?"

"Oops. Sorry, I wasn't paying attention."

He chuckled. "That sounds familiar."

Nicole's face burned and not from the exertion of going uphill. She coughed several times and tried to ignore the tightening in her chest. "I know you're a detective in Portland, but is it normal for cops to work at other police departments like you're doing?" She concentrated on taking controlled breaths.

"It's not unheard of, but not the norm either. Sometimes we are loaned to other places, but this job is different. I actually applied and went through the interview process the same as anyone else would. My position in Portland will be waiting for me in September."

The grocery store/gas station was in sight. Good thing too because her legs had turned to jelly. Since getting caught not pedaling, she hadn't quit pumping. They crossed Cottonwood Road and stopped at the air machine. "You want something to drink?" She slid off the bike.

"How about a bottle of water?"

"Okay. Be right back." On noodle legs she walked inside. Bike riding had sounded like a good idea, but now not so much. She chose Vitamin Water for herself and a plain H2O for Mark, paid then headed outside.

Her legs finally felt like they would hold as she strolled over to where Mark stood talking with a family. "All set?"

Mark nodded and took the water she offered, then stuffed it in one of the bottle holders on the frame of the bike. He turned back to the family. "Good to meet you, and remember to watch for the signs on the trails. As long as you stay on the right color path you shouldn't get lost." Mark straddled the bike and looked over his shoulder. "Where to?"

"My place. I'm thinking about that hill we coasted down. It's going to be a killer to get back up, and I'm not feeling well."

"You really do sound like you're coming down with something. How about you wait here, and I'll ride to your house on my own and come back for you with my car."

She looked around the gas station/mini-mart parking lot, and considered his suggestion. If she allowed him to go get the car, he'd think she was a wimp. "No. I'll be okay."

"If you're sure." He turned the bike in the direction they'd come and pedaled off. "That first day I was on duty, I thought my legs would give out more than once. At least I didn't have any serious hills to patrol."

Nicole studied Mark's muscular back. They'd be leaving Sunriver at about the same time. She couldn't help the attraction she felt toward him, and spending time with him drew her to him even more. Today had been a bad idea! All this sunshine and warm weather must be messing with her mind.

"You still with me back there?" He glanced over his shoulder.

"I'm helping."

"Not what I meant. You're so quiet. Everything okay? If you're feeling worse, we can walk the bike up the hill."

"I'm fine. Just thinking." She dug in and pedaled hard to the crest. Pain shot through her chest. Her breath came in short gasps. "Must . . . stop."

Mark pulled off the path and angled toward her. "You okay?"

She shook her head and tried to breathe, but her lungs wouldn't cooperate. Pulling in short shallow breaths, she prayed for God's help.

Mark touched her back. "Nicole?"

"Asthma attack." The words were barely out of her mouth before she sank to the dirt on the edge of the path. Her eyes watered. She hadn't had an attack like this since she was a child and didn't know what to do. She never carried her emergency inhaler.

"WHERE'S YOUR INHALER?"

"Home."

Mark's heart slammed against his chest. Why would someone with bad asthma not carry an emergency inhaler? Now was not the time for a medical emergency. He looked around for help. A few houses were nearby, but there was no guarantee they were occupied.

Nicole seemed to struggle to get even a little air. At least she hadn't passed out—yet.

Precious seconds ticked by as he tried to figure out what to do.

A group of kids rode up on their bikes. "She okay?" A girl asked.

"No. She's having an asthma attack. Do any of you have an emergency inhaler?" He looked from the girl to the others riding with her.

A boy who looked around fourteen pulled something from his pocket. "I have Albuterol. I've never used it, but my mom makes me carry it." He handed it to Mark, who in turn passed it to Nicole.

With tears in her eyes, she depressed the canister. An eternity seemed to pass before she repeated the process. She took a shaky breath then another. Finally, she breathed deeply. "Thanks." She handed the boy his medicine. "That'll teach me to go riding without my inhaler. I'll pay for a replacement."

"You're welcome. Like I said, I've never even used it. Don't worry about buying me a new one. My inhalers always end up expiring unused. I always thought it was stupid that my mom made me carry mine, but now I'm glad. You okay?"

"I am, thanks to you and your mom. Be sure to tell her I said thank you."

The boy grinned. "Okay. 'Bye."

The kids took off, leaving Mark alone with Nicole. He sat on the pavement, his feet resting in the dirt. "Lady, I've seen my share of emergencies, and though that didn't come close to the worst, you really had me scared."

"Sorry."

Mark thought about Tracy and the bomb that had taken her life. Nicole's asthma might not be a bomb but could have been as deadly.

Nicole's concerned eyes searched his face.

He squeezed her hand. "Don't look at me like that. You're the one who could have died."

"I wasn't going to die, but thanks for your help. That was a little disconcerting."

He nodded. Too bad he couldn't have stopped Tracy from picking up that bag with the homemade bomb inside.

"You have a haunted look in your eyes, and it's scaring me. What are you thinking about?"

"Nothing good. You ready to go?"

Nicole eyed him, frowning. "I wish you wouldn't do that. Sometimes sharing what's bothering you eases the burden of carrying it alone. I'd like to help."

He pulled her to standing, their faces inches apart. His gaze locked on hers. "Thank you for caring." The sounds around them faded as he brushed a strand of hair from her face and tucked it behind her ear. He lowered his mouth and brushed his lips across hers.

Her eyes fluttered, and she grinned. "Nice deflection."

He chuckled. "Not the response I was going for." He took her hand. "You up to riding back?"

"Maybe we should walk."

"Okay." He stood on one side of the bike and she the other. "Why don't you carry an emergency inhaler?"

"I've never needed one. I guess that's not entirely true. I haven't needed to use one in so long that I didn't think to bring it. Like that boy who helped me, mine always expire unused."

He nodded. "I guess I get that, but you take a risk not keeping it with you."

"My asthma is under control. I never have attacks. Well, I haven't since I was a teen. One thing is certain, I'll be carrying it with me from now on. I think my allergies set off this attack."

His gut tightened at the casual way she approached her

health. He cared about her and didn't want her taking unnecessary risks with her well-being, but from her perspective her reasoning made sense. "You mentioned having allergies?"

"Yes. They are usually mild, but not today."

"I've noticed." He shot her a teasing grin.

They walked in silence for the next twenty minutes until Nicole's cabin came into view. They cut through the foliage on a worn path.

"Home sweet home." Nicole opened the garage door. "Thanks for today. And sorry about earlier."

Mark touched a hand to her cheek. "No need to apologize. In spite of your asthma attack I had fun this afternoon."

"Me too."

"I have tomorrow off also. Maybe we could get together and do something? I'm thinking something water related."

She hesitated a moment then nodded. "I'd like that." A smile reached her beautiful eyes.

He let out the breath he'd been holding. He liked this woman—a lot.

CHAPTER SIXTEEN

NICOLE STRETCHED, ARCHING HER BACK, AND kicked off the covers. She'd dreamed about Mark last night and relived his kiss over and over. What was she doing? She couldn't help being drawn to Mark, but how could they ever have a lasting relationship with her aversion to big and congested cities and the fact that he put his life on the line every time he put on his uniform.

Confusion knotted her stomach. Maybe she should call him and cancel, because the more time she spent with him the more she liked him.

She squinted at the sunlight streaming in through the bedroom window and breathed in deeply the scent of fresh brewed coffee that wafted from the kitchen. Oh the joys of having a programmable coffee maker. Glancing at the bedside clock, she gasped. Mark would be there in fifteen minutes. No time to cancel now, it would be rude, and she couldn't treat him that way after he'd been so kind.

She darted to the bathroom and banging her toe into the doorframe, she sucked in a breath. This was not a good way to start a day that held such promise. Hopefully it wasn't a sign of things to come. Tears of pain and frustration pricked her eyes.

Closing her eyes, she shot off a quick prayer. She had been praying since coming to Sunriver, and thanks to Sarah's invite to church, she'd begun to rekindle her relationship with the Lord. Grams would be pleased. She winced at her throbbing toe. No way would she allow this to ruin her day. She stood putting pressure on her foot and gasped. Who would've thought a tiny toe could cause so much pain? She limped to the sink and splashed water on her face, doing her best to ignore the throbbing. After running her fingers through her hair to get out the tangles, she slipped on the black swimsuit from Grams then topped it off with a tank top under a red button-up blouse and khaki shorts. Her reflection in the mirror startled her. She appeared . . . happy even if she was in pain.

She peered down again at her red and swollen toe and sighed. It really looked ugly. She tried to move it and gritted her teeth against the groan that pressed at her throat. Hopefully the swimsuit meant they'd be in cool water, which would soothe the pain and maybe bring down the swelling.

Pain or not, no way could she make it through the day without coffee. She hop-walked to the kitchen, being careful to avoid putting much pressure on her right foot. After pouring a mug full and adding vanilla flavored creamer, she sat and savored the rich aroma for a moment. A quick glance at the clock above the stove prompted her to gulp it down. She still needed makeup!

Reaching into her purse, she pulled out the essentials and applied tinted sunblock to her face, a touch of lipstick, then brushed on a light dusting of powder. She gave a mental shrug. "That will have to do." She transferred the important stuff into a hobo bag and dropped it onto the counter.

A knock at the door drew her away from the kitchen. "Coming!" She hobbled as fast as possible then pulled the door open.

Mark's face lit, and her heart rate kicked up a notch. He looked like he'd stepped off the cover of a sports magazine with his khaki shorts, dark sunglasses and rafting sandals. "Good morning. You ready?"

"Just about. Be right back." She turned toward the bathroom again and moved forward trying desperately not to limp.

"What happened?" The concern in Mark's voice stopped her. He sidled up to her and knelt beside her foot. "That looks painful."

"It's nothing." She looked down at the cause of her embarrassment. "My little toe collided with the door frame this morning.

He frowned. "Is it broken?"

"I couldn't tell."

"Let me look. I've broken my fair share of bones."

Her lips twitched. "So you're a doctor too, huh?"

A slow smile lifted his lips, and he settled his hands at her waist. "Up you go."

Before she realized what was happening, he'd lifted her onto the counter. Good grief the man was strong! She was no lightweight. He squatted before her and took her foot in his hand. She caught her breath. Her gaze trekked down from his face to his hands as they gently probed her injury. "Careful." She winced when he touched an especially tender spot.

"I think you'll live. It might be broken, but it's hard to say. Do you have any tape?"

"I don't think so."

"In that case, I'll have to carry you."

"What? No. I can walk."

He scooped her into his arms before she could protest further. Her heart tripped into a staccato beat. She reached for her bag.

"You have everything?" He spoke softly inches from her face.

Her cheeks had to match the color of her top. "My flip flops are by the door."

"I'll come back for them." Somehow he opened the door without dropping her and managed to maneuver through without bumping her foot. He gently deposited her on the hood of his car.

He chuckled. "Sorry, I didn't think this through. I should've opened the door before bringing you out here." Sadie barked from the backseat.

"But then I'd have been right behind you, and it wouldn't have mattered."

He grinned and strode off for her flip-flops.

She sat stunned for a moment before gathering her wits and scrambling into the car. To say he had surprised her was an understatement, but boy she liked his kind of surprises. Had he heard her heart pounding when he held her close? She shook off the embarrassing thought and watched him jog back to the car.

Sadie whined for attention.

Nicole turned and scratched behind the dog's ear. "You're a good girl."

The driver's side door opened, and he slid in. "All set?"

"Yes." She glanced at him. "You do realize you can't carry me all day?"

"No worries. I have tape in my gym bag."

"If you had it all along why didn't you . . ."

He shot a mischievous look her way. "I'll tape it when we get there. Were you sleepwalking or something?"

"Not exactly. I overslept and wasn't paying enough attention."

"At least we won't be walking much today." He started the engine and pulled out.

"I was hoping that would be the case since you said to wear my swimsuit." Looking out the side window, she mentally mapped where they were. "When do I get to know what you have planned?"

"We're going canoeing. Spencer has a canoe and offered to let us borrow it. He'll meet us at the river and will pick us up at the takeout point in a few hours."

The image of the officer dressed in drag brought a smile to her lips. "That's nice of him." Then another thought struck her — the last time she was in a boat her oar broke. Hopefully there would be no repeat of that incident today.

MARK PULLED THE CAR to a stop on the side of the road. The river wouldn't be crowded this time of day. The chill in the air made him grateful he'd worn a hoodie. But the clear sky would soon allow the sun to warm them.

"Stay put, Nicole. I'll be right back." He grabbed athletic tape from his gym bag and pulled open the passenger door. She looked at him with worry in her eyes.

"I think it'll be fine. I don't need that."

He shook his head and squatted then rested her foot on his knee. "Sorry, but you'll be getting in and out of the canoe, and I'd feel better knowing your toe is protected at least a little. I'll be gentle."

"This is going to hurt isn't it?" Nicole squeezed her eyes shut. "I can't watch."

He chuckled. You'd think he was sticking her with a needle or something. He ripped off a couple inches of tape, then split it down the center. "Okay. I'm going to tape your toe to the one next to it."

She nodded. "Please hurry."

The tension in her voice made his brow furrow. Hopefully she wouldn't kick him. He quickly taped her toes. "All done."

She slowly opened her eyes and looked at her foot. "Really?"

"Yes. Wasn't so bad was it?" He gently removed her foot from his knee and stood.

"Thanks. Sorry for being such a baby. I've never been a good patient."

"Remind me to call 911 and let the EMT's deal with you the next time you hurt yourself." He shot her a teasing grin.

"There won't be a next time. I don't make a habit of injuring myself." She shielded her eyes against the morning sun. "Is that

Spencer?" She nodded toward a pickup that pulled up behind them.

"Yes. You ready?"

She slipped on her flip-flops then stepped out gingerly. "It doesn't hurt as much now." She hoisted her bag onto her shoulder.

"I'm glad." He snagged her hand and gently squeezed it.

Sadie hopped out and loped over to Spencer.

They walked hand in hand to Spencer's rig where he leaned against the front grille. "Morning!" He dropped Nicole's hand and shook Spencer's. "Thanks for this."

"No problem. But now we're even for the other night."

"Ha. Not yet. I was up for thirty-six hours because of that stakeout."

Spencer shook his head. "Give me a hand." He walked to the back and together they removed the canoe from the bed and carried it to the entry point.

Nicole followed silently.

"Okay. I'll see you both in a few hours. Call me if you need a ride sooner." Spencer looked to Nicole. "Any more problems out your way?"

"Thankfully no." She bit her lower lip. "At least not that I noticed. I've been away from the house much of the time. Do you think the burglars robbed any of the other houses on my street?"

"Nothing's been reported by the owners or any property management companies." He glanced toward Mark. "Relax and have a good time today. Sorry I brought it up." Spencer handed them each a life vest, which they slipped on.

"Hop in, Sadie," Mark said from the riverbank.

His dog leaped into the canoe causing it to teeter from side to side, but Mark quickly steadied it. "Easy, girl."

Sadie settled onto the bottom of the metal canoe looking at Nicole eagerly.

Nicole chuckled. "I'm coming." She carefully stepped in then slipped past Sadie and sat on the front bench seat as Mark held the vessel steady.

Satisfied she was secure, he grabbed the cooler he'd packed then stepped in. "Thanks, Spencer. We'll meet you at the other end."

"Have fun." Spencer pushed them off with one final wave and walked away.

Wide-eyed, Nicole looked over her shoulder at Mark. "Umm. What am I supposed to do?"

The canoe wobbled from side to side. After Mark gave her a mini lesson, on bows, sterns, paddling and back paddling, they set a course for the middle of the slow moving river. "We could float along and enjoy the scenery for a while if you'd like. We have plenty of time."

"Sounds good to me." She took her phone from her bag and pulled up the camera app. "I want to remember this summer forever." Reeds along the bank swayed in the breeze as she focused in and clicked off several shots. A speedboat flew by. Nicole gripped the sides of the canoe and yelped. "Are we going to tip?"

"Not if I can help it." Mark maneuvered the canoe to a better angle and glared after the boat. Some people were beyond rude. The wake from the boat continued to rock the canoe, but not as severely as before.

Nicole dropped her phone to her lap and gripped the side of the canoe, her eyes large with fear. "You sure we aren't going to tip? I suppose this is why you said to wear my swimsuit."

The canoe finally stopped rocking. "Not exactly. I'd planned to go white water rafting, but it didn't work out, so Spencer came to the rescue early this morning. I didn't think to call and tell you not to wear a swimsuit. But if you'd like to take a swim . . ." The water would probably be cold, but he doubted that would stop her if she really wanted to take a dip.

"No. That's okay." Nicole released her grip on the canoe.

"That was nice of him. He always seems so serious. I'm surprised he owns a canoe."

Mark chuckled. "You don't know Spencer. After a full night doing surveillance you get to know a person. He's a good guy."

Spencer's frustration over this case would probably come to a head soon. They must've spooked the perpetrators because there hadn't been any more burglaries reported. Maybe they wised up and decided to leave before they were caught. "Is your asthma okay today?"

"Yes. I'm so embarrassed about yesterday. I've been practically symptom free since I was a teen. I guess the combination of allergies and exercise set it off." She sneezed as if their conversation had ordered the reaction.

"We'll take it easy. I'd hate to have a repeat out here on the water." He directed them toward an inlet.

"I agree, but I brought my inhaler, so don't worry." She looked over her shoulder. "Any chance I could turn around and face you? This is awkward."

"Sure, I thought we'd stop for breakfast as soon as I see a good spot. When you get back in you can go ahead and face me." He searched the grassy bank and steered toward the shoreline.

With a strong thrust, Mark propelled them to the edge of the soft bank. He craned his neck and spotted a log on a flat spot. "This looks like a great place to picnic."

"I agree." She stood and stepped out. "I'm glad we're eating. I didn't have time for breakfast, and I'm a breakfast kind of girl."

Mark retrieved the cooler and followed her to the log. "I aim to please." He sat and slid the lid off, revealing fresh fruit, blueberry muffins, milk, and bottles of water.

"Yum. You thought of everything." Nicole pulled out an apple. The crisp crunch of the fruit was loud in the morning stillness.

The gentle flow of the river made rippling sounds along the bank. An osprey soared overhead and landed on the top of a pine tree. The wildlife alone made for the perfect morning, but the company couldn't be beat either. Nicole was so different than he'd first imagined when they'd met on that traffic circle.

The screech of an eagle drew his gaze. He glanced at Nicole, her chin tipped up and her lips parted slightly. He suppressed a smile. "Pretty amazing huh?"

She closed her mouth and nodded. "I've never been out here. When I was a kid, we mostly stayed on the trails around the lodge and village."

"You and your grandmother?"

"No, my parents and brother and I would come here every summer." A shadow crossed her face. "Grams didn't bring me here."

"You never talk about your family."

"This summer has made me think about what happened more than ever. I've avoided it since I was a kid, but meeting you has brought it all to the surface."

He jerked his head back slightly. "Me? Why?"

Nicole sighed and bit her bottom lip. "I'm going to tell you something I never talk about. But I don't want to discuss it, or answer any questions. Okay?"

He nodded, sensing that even the sound of his voice might silence her.

"When I was ten my brother was killed as the result of a high speed police chase. He was in the wrong place at the wrong time. The man who hit him robbed a bank, then carjacked a woman's car." Her voice caught, and her gaze slammed into his. "That man survived, but Robbie was killed instantly when the car he was riding in was T-boned on the passenger's side. The police came to our house. I was standing behind my dad when they told him what had happened. My dad had a massive heart-attack right there. They gave him CPR until an ambulance came, but it was too late, and they couldn't get his heart to start."

She took a drink from a water bottle and stared off toward

the river. Her voice lowered. "I watched my dad die. Then a week later I came home from school and found my mom dead in the bathroom—suicide." She dried her eyes on a napkin. "In a matter of a week I lost my entire family. All except Grams." She angled her head down.

He swallowed hard. Hurt for the child she was, and pain for the woman she'd become, strangled him. He gulped down a half-bottle of water then took her hand and cradled it between his. There were no words.

She squared her shoulders and slipped her hand from his. "You ready to go?"

"Sure." He stood and offered her a hand up. They stood so close he could feel her warm breath on his neck. He folded his arms around her and pulled her close. "Thank you for trusting me." Mark now understood the look of sadness he'd seen shadowing her eyes from time to time.

A WHISPER OF DOUBT warned Nicole. She'd better tread carefully. Her heart was quickly becoming entangled with Mark's. Another heartbreak would be tough to handle, but it felt so good to be in his arms—safe, at least for now. But he'd return to his big city job at the end of the summer, get caught up in some case and forget all about her. She watched television. Detectives were married to their jobs. Her ex-boyfriend accused her of the same thing—ironic, but if she had a man like Mark in her life that would change.

What was she thinking? She stepped out of his embrace. It could never work between them. "We should go before Spencer calls out a search party." Sadie leaned against her leg and nuzzled her nose against Nicole's hand. She squatted and hugged the sweet animal. Tension melted from her.

Mark gathered their trash and she grabbed the cooler before

stepping carefully back into the canoe. Sadie followed and then he pushed off and set their course. "You're quiet."

"I'm thinking about the future."

"That's kind of vague?"

"Exactly! It's a mystery, and I don't like that."

Mark chuckled. "For I know the plans I have for you," declares the Lord, "plans to prosper you and not to harm you, plans to give you hope and a future."

"I've heard that before. What is it?"

"Jeremiah 29:11."

She pursed her lips. "I wish He'd tell me what those plans are because I feel lost."

"If you ask Him to, He will. It might not be today or even soon, but He will guide you."

"That sure would be nice. I hate not knowing my future."

"Don't we all. But for me it's enough that He knows. I try to pay attention, so I don't miss out on His plan for me."

"Too bad He doesn't send us emails with instructions." She shook her head and did a double take toward the bank. "Look. There's a deer." She held up her phone and rose up on her knees. The canoe rocked from side to side. "Okay, that was a bad idea. Sorry." She carefully scooted back to her perch and pressed her lips tightly together.

Mark chortled. "Another stunt like that, and we'll both be swimming."

"At least we're dressed for it." She shot him a cheeky grin then suddenly frowned as a worried look filled her eyes.

"What's the matter?"

"Nothing, but—there are fish in the water right?"

"Of course."

"I only like fish on my plate, not around my toes."

Mark tossed his head back and belly laughed.

Nicole smacked a paddle through the water, drenching his torso.

"Lady, this means war." He slapped the paddle in the river and sent water flying, drenching her head to foot.

Sadie barked at them.

"That's cold!" She pulled a towel from her bag and wiped her face. "Not nice, Mister."

"You started it."

"You're right. Sorry."

"I'm not. The look on your face when I retaliated was priceless." A cluster of people were shouting at them from the riverbank and waving their arms. In the midst of their water fight, they'd drifted to the other side of the river. He looked forward and gasped. "Nicole, don't panic, but we need to turn the canoe around and head across the river before things get a little choppy. I need you to face forward carefully and help me get this to shore."

NICOLE SLID AROUND ON the canoe's bench seat as gracefully as possible without tipping them over. The calm river came to an abrupt change ahead. Her heart raced. "I sure hope you know what you're doing, because I don't have a clue."

Mark shouted orders, and she followed. Within seconds they had the canoe heading in the correct direction. She dug in deep and paddled against the current. Spencer stood on the bank at their pullout spot. He stepped onto a rock and reached toward them.

Nicole paddled with all her strength until Spencer had grabbed the canoe and pulled it onto the bank. She took his hand and jumped from the canoe, wincing when she landed on the foot with the injured toe. She perched on a large boulder and watched the men remove the canoe from the river and carry it to Spencer's long-bed pickup.

Mark and Spencer razzed each other all the way. Nicole grinned and leaned on her elbows. She closed her eyes, listening to the children's playful screams, reminding her of the water fight a short time ago.

"You ready?"

Nicole jumped. "Mark, you startled me."

He chuckled and scooted beside her. "Spencer needs to get going. He'll drop us at my car."

"Okay."

He reached his arms toward her. "Come on. I'll help you so you don't aggravate your toe."

She leaned toward him and allowed his strength to guide her safely off the boulder. Mark wrapped his warm hand around hers. Her fingers tingled for the second time that day. She caught her breath, and her gaze darted to his face.

He raised a brow. "Everything okay?"

"Uh-huh."

"Good. You think we could get together again sometime? Seems to me I still owe you a night on the town."

She nodded. "Sure, any time. My schedule is open." Now why had she said that? It was only prolonging the inevitable since they had no future together, but one look at the grin on his face warmed her from the inside out. What was one more date?

CHAPTER SEVENTEEN

M ARK STOOD BESIDE SPENCER'S DESK AT the PD. He disconnected the call from Sarah and stuffed his cell phone into his pocket. His mind told him not to panic, but his gut said he needed to check on Connor.

"Everything okay?" Spencer glanced his way and popped a chip into his mouth. "What's the problem now?"

"Connor didn't check in with Sarah like he was supposed to, and he's not answering the house phone, or his cell phone. She's tried texting him, but got no response."

Concern etched Spencer's eyes. "You think he's in trouble?"

"I don't know, but I should head over to his place to be safe. He has a gift for finding mischief."

Spencer shook his head. "Any chance you could ask Nicole to check in on him? I could use you here. This case is driving me nuts. I feel like we're missing something."

"I'd rather deal with Connor myself. I'll be back in less than twenty minutes."

"What if he's not there?"

"One problem at a time, Spencer." He grabbed his keys and headed to his car. Five minutes later he pulled up to Sarah's house, killed the engine and approached the house. Everything from the outside looked okay. He knocked then listened for noise inside and heard nothing.

His unease grew. Sarah said Connor was supposed to be hanging out at home today. Where was he? He walked toward the back of the house and peered in through the slider—no one to be seen. *Now what?*

He turned and slowly scanned the area. The tree limbs were up too high for him to reach, so Connor wouldn't be up a tree, and there wasn't any brush nearby to hide in since Sarah and her neighbors kept the landscape clear.

He rubbed his chin. If I were a twelve-year-old boy, where would I go?

His cell buzzed. "Hey, Spencer."

"He there?"

"If he is, he's not answering."

"Did you try opening the door?"

"Uh, no." He pulled on the slider and sure enough, it opened. "Thanks. I'm going inside."

"I'll stay on the line."

He pulled the phone away from his face. "Connor!" He moved from the kitchen into the hall that led to the bedrooms—still no one. "I'm heading upstairs to the loft," he said into the phone. He climbed the steep spiral stairs. At the top he stopped. Connor laid sprawled on the floor. His head rested against a beanbag and a book lay across his chest. "Found him. I'm going to hang up."

"Glad he's okay. Hurry back."

"Yep." He sent Sarah a text assuring her all was well with Connor, then nudged the toe of his shoe against the boy's leg.

Connor jerked, and his eyes flew open. "Mark? What are you doing here?"

"You weren't answering your phone so Sarah asked me to check on you."

"She's such a worrywart—even worse than my mom." He pushed up then plopped onto the beanbag with a yawn. "What time is it?"

"A little past one o'clock."

"Oh wow, I slept a long time. I didn't even eat lunch." He smacked his arm across his midsection.

Mark chuckled. Clearly the kid was fine if he was concerned about his stomach. "Okay then, I'm out of here. Keep your cell nearby next time you're up here."

"It's in my pocket." He pulled it out and looked at the screen. "Dead. I guess I forgot to charge it."

Mark ruffled his hair. "I'll see you." He strode from the house and paused at the slider. "Hey, Connor!"

"Yeah?"

"Lock up."

"Okay."

"Now." He waited until the boy trotted down the stairs.

"Mark?"

"Hmm?"

"Why'd you come looking for me? I know Sarah called, but you didn't have to."

"You're my friend, Connor, and friends look out for each other. If you were in trouble, I wanted to be here for you."

The boy's eyes clouded, and he cleared his throat. "Thanks."

"No problem." Clearly Connor wasn't accustomed to being looked out for. He felt bad for the boy. "You want to shoot hoops tonight?"

"Really?"

He nodded. "I can pick you up at six."

"No need. Sarah and Nicole are playing tennis in the courts nearby."

A smiled tugged at his lips. "Perfect. See you then." He slid the glass door open and left. Tonight should prove to be fun. Plus, he'd get to see Nicole again.

NICOLE DABBED HER FACE with a towel as she walked toward the net and Sarah. "You win. Should we do a cool down lap around the field? My toe isn't bothering me much anymore. I don't think it was broken after all."

"Sure, we can leave our gear with Connor and Mark."

"Great idea." She'd been hoping for a chance to say hi to Mark. She slipped her racket into the bag and strolled beside her friend to the basketball court.

Mark stood at the free throw line and released the ball— *swish*. He glanced toward them and grinned. "Game over?"

"Yes," Nicole pointed to their equipment. "Would you keep an eye on our stuff while we walk a cool down lap?"

"Sure." He waved.

Sarah grinned, and they walked toward the trail. "The two of you make a cute couple."

"Thanks, but like I said we aren't a couple. What about you? Is there a man in your life?"

"I wish. There's a guy at church I've had my eye on, but he doesn't know I exist."

"You should introduce yourself."

Sarah wrinkled her nose. "Believe it or not, I'm kind of shy when it comes to guys. Speaking of which, Connor can't stop talking about your man. From the time I arrived home today it's been Mark this and Mark that."

Nicole ignored the comment about Mark being her man. "Why is your cousin so infatuated with him?"

Sarah explained how she hadn't been able to reach Connor that afternoon, panicked, and called Mark.

"Why didn't you call me?"

"I was afraid he was really in trouble, Mark's a cop, and I didn't want to involve you if there was any danger."

"Wow, you must've been scared out of your mind."

"I was a little nuts, but Mark checked on him right away and discovered Connor had fallen asleep, and his phone was dead."

"I'm glad it turned out okay. I imagine that's one of the reasons Connor likes him so much."

"I'm sure of it. The man has rescued the kid on a number of occasions this summer, and he's shown an interest in him. Connor needed that, especially since his own dad is a flake."

"Mark mentioned something about that." They'd looped around the park and ended at the basketball court.

Mark jogged over to them with Connor by his side. "All finished?"

"Yes," Sarah said. "It's time to hit the shower." She clamped a hand onto Connor's shoulder and steered him toward her car. "See you," she called over her shoulder.

Mark tossed the ball up then caught it. "Care to shoot some hoops?"

"I'm not very good."

"Doesn't matter." He bounce-passed the ball to her.

Her stomach did a little flip. She flashed her best smile, then dribbled the ball while walking in a circle. "I heard about what happened with Connor today. You've really made an impression on him." She stopped dribbling and propelled the ball in the direction of the hoop—colossal miss.

Mark chased after the ball and brought it back. "The kid needs a man in his life. I did too at his age."

He had alluded to this before, and Nicole sensed he might be willing to share his story. "I'm tired, do you mind if we sit?" She walked toward a shaded picnic table, hoping he'd follow. She plopped onto the tabletop and rested her feet on the bench seat. "If you're willing, I'd love to hear why it is that you can relate so well to Connor."

Mark sat beside her and stared vacantly ahead. "I suppose it's only fair after what you shared with me." He pulled a towel from his bag and wiped his face. "I was angry and heading down the wrong path when I met Sam."

"Sam?"

"A cop that lived a few doors down from me. He caught me spray painting his garbage cans one night."

"What happened?"

"For starters he made me clean those cans inside and out. I had to wait until the garbage was collected the next morning to do the inside, but Sam wouldn't let me get away with not following through." He chuckled and flicked a glance her way. "He actually came to my house the next day and told me the cans were empty and to hustle up. Man, those things stunk. I think it was the first time they'd been washed out and they were *old*." He ran a hand across his nose as if he could still smell the stench.

"Then what happened?"

"Sam dragged a lawn chair to the front yard and talked to me the whole time I cleaned."

"About what?"

"Beats me." He shook his head. "It didn't matter what he said, but that he took the time to be with me, which was more than my dad ever did." He rested his elbows on his knees. "I think he was the first grownup to ever make me feel important."

"Wow. Is he the reason you became a cop?"

Mark nodded, then pushed up and off the table. "Want to grab a bite to eat in the village? My treat." He raised a brow.

"I'm all sweaty and need to clean up."

"Me too. I'll meet you at the Village Bar & Grill in an hour."

"I loved their burgers when I was a kid. I haven't been there in forever." She stood and walked beside him to the parking lot. Parting ways at the end of the summer would be difficult at best. The more time she spent with the man, the more she wanted to be with him, but that was impossible.

CHAPTER EIGHTEEN

NICOLE SAT AT A TABLE ON the deck outside the Village Bar & Grill watching a little brown bird hop across the deck, presumably in search of scraps. A light breeze made her glad she'd thought to grab a sweater on her way out the door. Mark strolled around the corner of the building. His face brightened when their eyes collided, and she lifted a hand.

Mark pulled out a chair and sat. "Have you been waiting long?"

"Only long enough to be seated and enjoy the scenery."

"It's nice out here."

She nodded and handed him the menu.

"I know what I want."

"Perfect, because I'm starving." A short time later they placed their orders. She grinned and admired his dark chocolate-colored eyes—so much depth, yet mysterious at the same time. She looked away and fingered her napkin when she realized she was staring. "I'm glad you suggested this. I usually hole up in my house in the evenings. I forget how pleasant it is in the village during the dinner hour."

"Yeah, it's nice."

Her cell phone rang. "Sorry." She pulled it out and noted the number was a local area code. "I'm really sorry, Mark, but I think I should take this call."

"Go ahead."

"Thanks for understanding." She pressed accept. "This is Nicole." She listened as the woman on the other end introduced herself as the principal of the elementary school in Sunriver and explained she'd like her to come in for an interview. They finalized the plans, and she stuffed the phone into her purse. "I can't believe it! I finally got an interview, and it's local."

"That's great. Congratulations!"

"Thanks." Her mind buzzed with a riot of thoughts. What she would wear topped the list. Good thing she'd packed a skirt and several professional looking tops.

"How's the hunt coming along? Speaking of which, I still owe you a night on the town."

She shook her head. "You don't have to."

"I know. I *want* to. Have you found any new clues?"

"For what?" Her scattered thoughts created chaos in her mind and frustrated her. She should know what he was talking about.

He chuckled. "You know, the reason you're in Sunriver."

"Oh yeah. Sorry, my mind is going a mile a minute." She took a cleansing breath and focused on the handsome man. "Okay. I'm back." She shot him a cheeky grin. "The game is stalled. I'm at a loss. I know it isn't over, but I'm clueless—no pun intended."

He grinned.

Their orders arrived. Nicole breathed in the heavenly scent of her bacon cheeseburger.

Mark offered a blessing for the food, and they dug into their mouthwatering burgers. A short time later, he leaned back and laced his fingers across his midsection. "Tell me more about yourself, Nicole. What's your passion in life? And don't say working."

She laughed. "You know me so well."

"Come on, don't evade the question." He leaned forward then reached across the table and took her hand.

She may as well lay it all on him and see what happened. "I allowed my social life to disappear, got dumped by my boyfriend because I'm boring and have no life outside of work. Basically I'm jobless, clueless, and . . ." She tried to think of a word to rhyme and came up empty. "And not a poet."

"I know all of that." He winked. "Why do you teach, and why were you taking care of your grandmother on your own rather than hiring a medical professional?" He stroked her hand with his thumb as his words rolled softly off his lips.

"I'm a teacher because I want to make a difference, and in my opinion the best way to do that is with children. I love watching their faces light up when they finally understand a math problem and listening to them giggle when I read them a funny story. Kids are fun. Sure there are the ones that make me re-think my decision to spend so much time with children, but then there are the rest who confirm I'm making a difference."

"What about your grandma?"

Nicole studied her empty plate for a moment. "Hiring someone to take care of her never crossed my mind. Grams didn't have anyone but me. My dad was her only child, and I was happy to be there for her. We were close when I was a kid, and she was always my rock, so I wanted to be that for her."

He nodded. "I figured it was something like that. I'm glad you had her in your life. It's important to have someone to look up to."

"And that's what you are for Connor. At least for the summer."

"Exactly, but I figure we can Skype once I'm back in Portland. In this techno world we live in there's no reason to lose touch."

She nodded. Skyping might be good enough for Connor, but it wasn't for her. A knot settled in her stomach. Her heart had become entangled with Mark's, and she didn't know what to do about it. She could never be happy living in a big city like Portland.

LATER THAT EVENING, NICOLE climbed the stairs to the loft in her rental. Thankfully, the remodel was finished and had turned out lovely. The owners would be thrilled when they saw it.

She stared at the floor-to-ceiling bookshelf. Now where was that book? Grams had mentioned in a note that her favorite book was here, and something about the way she'd worded her note, led Nicole to think it was important that she find the book. She'd procrastinated enough, it was time to finish the game and let Grams rest in peace once and for all.

She read title after title and couldn't find one that stuck out. She frowned and squatted to check out the lower titles—nothing that tugged at her memory. Maybe she should bring up a sturdy chair to stand on and start from the top. No, that didn't make sense. Grams wouldn't have put it so high she couldn't reach it. Maybe it was time to tear this bookshelf apart book by book and thumb through each one, because clearly she was getting nowhere with her current method.

In truth, she'd been stalling, enjoying the summer. Enjoying her new friends, especially Mark. If she found this book would all the fun end? She didn't want life to go back to the way it had been. But, it was time. She needed to finish this.

She sat forward on her knees and looked around the small space with only enough room for the bookcase, lamp and a single recliner. The tip of a piece of paper poked out from under the recliner. She grasped it and sat in the chair.

I hope you figured out by now the game has begun. You are well on your way to discovering one of life's great gifts. Enjoy being pampered at the spa. I've arranged for you to receive a facial, manicure, and pedicure.

Be watching for the next clue. It may arrive when or where you least expect it. I will give you one clue in case you get out of order. Home is where the heart is.

Xoxo, Grams

Nicole gazed out over her summer home. Clearly this page had been separated from the note she'd found taped to the chair when she'd first arrived. A smile tipped her mouth. Another clue, but this one she really needed to think about. Good thing Grams had anticipated trouble finding the clue, because until this moment, the game had been stalled.

She clambered to her feet and rested her elbows on the loft railing. What does 'home is where the heart is' mean? It was a common saying, but the note seemed to be saying the next clue had to be someplace in the house. That clue probably told her exactly which book too! "But where?" And was it still here, or did the burglars inadvertently nab it?

MARK FOLLOWED SPENCER, WHO carried a laptop, into the conference room. Mark closed the door and leaned against the table. "What's going on?"

"Do you remember the day Nicole's house was burglarized?"

"Of course." Mark set his jaw.

Spencer opened the computer and pulled up a photo. "Do you recognize that woman?"

"Sure. She goes to my church. Her name is Sarah. What's this have to do with Nicole?"

Spencer changed the screen and pulled up a timeline graph. "This is a progression of the burglaries." He pointed to the date. "That's a week-and-a-half before Nicole arrived, right?"

Mark nodded and frowned. What was Spencer getting at? He wouldn't, no couldn't try and pin this on Nicole—not again. There was no way she was responsible.

"I did some digging. Are you aware Nicole is unemployed?"

"Yes. She mentioned it."

"And did you know that her friend Sarah moonlights for one of the rental agencies here in the village?"

Mark's brows rose. That was news. "Where are you going with this?"

"Don't you even want to know what she does?"

"I figured you'd tell me," he said dryly. He wanted to wipe the smug grin off Spencer's face.

"She cleans their office two nights a week."

"Why doesn't their housecleaning staff do that?"

"They only clean the rental properties."

Mark rubbed his chin. If Sarah cleaned the office after hours, she'd have access to their records. "I think I see where you're going, but you're forgetting one major fact. Anyone can find out if a house is available to rent simply by checking online. In essence, they can tell if a house is occupied at any given time based on that information."

"True, but here's the interesting part. Nicole's place has a block on it for the entire summer. Didn't you say she came here on the spur of the moment?"

His stomach knotted. "Yes, that's what she told me." Could she have been faking being upset about the break in to fool them? He shook off the thought. He read people well, and Nicole was definitely the victim, not the perpetrator. Besides Grams probably anticipated she'd die before summer and reserved the house in Nicole's name knowing she'd honor her wishes and play along. Spencer was off base once again.

"I think I'm on to something." He frowned. "But two things bug me about my theory. Nicole has a squeaky clean record, and unless she's the best con artist around, it's difficult to imagine her capable of this."

"Exactly. You're wasting time and looking at the wrong person." Mark shook his head. How could Spencer veer so far off track? Surely he had to know Nicole had nothing to do with the break-ins. "Just because Sarah works after hours at the property management company does not make her guilty, and it absolutely doesn't implicate Nicole."

"Sarah has a record—DUI and shoplifting." Spencer clicked a button then scrolled down. "He pulled up a different picture. "Do these women look familiar?"

Mark leaned forward and nodded. He'd never forget the piranhas. "How do you connect them to Nicole?"

"She's friends with Sarah who is friends with these women."

Mark ran a hand through his hair. "No matter what Sarah's past is, Nicole is innocent. Let me talk to her and see what I can find out."

"No way. If she's in on this, she would tip off Sarah and her friends. That could explain why nothing happened the night we were at her place—she tipped them off."

"Ridiculous! And if Nicole is *innocent*, which she is, she can help us."

Spencer looked past his shoulder and seemed to be giving his opinion some thought. "If you're wrong—"

"I'm not." He knew Nicole and thought he had a good handle on Sarah, but her record took him by surprise. He'd seen her at church, talked with her on the phone a time or two regarding Connor. Nicole liked her, but he was also smart enough to realize people lived double lives. What if Sarah was putting on a show? It looked like he had a bit of detective work to do. He only hoped Nicole wouldn't get hurt in the process.

NICOLE APPLIED A COAT of berry colored lipstick and pressed her lips together. The dress Grams gave her fit perfectly. She slipped into the strappy sandals then grabbed her clutch. Mark would be here any minute to make good on his promise of a night on the town.

A knock on the door drew her. She pulled it open. "Hi, Mark."

"You look gorgeous." His eyes roved from her face to her heels then back up.

Her cheeks warmed, and she suspected they matched the color of her lipstick. "Thanks. You look nice too." His black trousers topped off with a white shirt, and a black and silver tie, enhanced his physique and reminded her of a G-man.

He flashed a smile and offered his arm. "I made reservations at Anthony's Restaurant in the Old Mill District."

"I've heard they have great seafood." She closed and locked the door behind them.

Mark ambled beside her toward the car. "How've you been?"

"Great. The remodel is finished, and the master suite is so luxurious!" She almost offered to show it to him later but quickly realized how that would sound. She cleared her throat. "Plus, I found a missing part of a clue from Grams that I'm trying to figure out, and the reading selection at the house is amazing. I think I've read three books since I last saw you. And best of all, I got a job! I had the interview this afternoon and was hired on the spot."

A grin lit his face. "I knew you would. I guess this is a celebration dinner."

"Call it whatever you want, but let's go. I'm starved."

"I like a woman who speaks her mind." He opened the door. "After you."

"I've been so keyed up since getting the job, I could barely function. You're the first person I've told." She slid into the passenger seat.

He jogged around to the driver's seat then got in. "Sarah doesn't even know?"

"Nope. Although I should call her soon. I haven't seen her

since last week."

"I guess that means you're not getting in any tennis with Sarah." He shot her a teasing grin.

"Not since the evening we had dinner together."

Mark's brow furrowed.

"Something wrong?"

"What? No." He frowned and shook his head. "Why do you ask?" He had both hands on the wheel as they zoomed up the entrance onto US 97.

"No reason. You seemed bothered for a moment."

Mark flashed a grin. "Nope. How well do you know Sarah?"

"Not very since our friendship is new." She tilted her head. "Why do you ask?"

"No reason." He kept his eyes on the road.

Nicole pressed her lips together. She'd spent enough time with the man to be able to read him a little, and he wasn't telling her something. Why would he want to know about Sarah? Oh well, she wouldn't allow it to ruin their date. "I've been looking forward to our dinner."

He flashed a grin in her direction. "Me too. Tell me about the clue you've been trying to figure out."

"It was a note that said, home is where the heart is."

"Hmm. Makes me think the clue is at your place. Have you searched your house?"

"Everywhere I can think to look."

"You must be missing something. Then again, maybe we're being too literal."

"What else could it mean?" Nicole didn't want to think about the game right now. She'd spent so much effort trying to figure out her grandma's clue, she needed a break, but Mark seemed to really enjoy the challenge, so she'd let him try to figure it out. Maybe he'd even succeed where she'd failed.

"Heart and home could be symbolic."

"Of what?" She turned toward him and almost laughed at

the look of concentration on his face. He was getting into the hunt.

"I'm not sure. But when I figure it out. I'll let you know. In the meantime, I think your grandma's scavenger hunt has been a success. Wasn't the point for you to relax and have fun? It seems to me she accomplished that and more."

Could it really be that simple? Her shoulders sagged. She'd expected some kind of hoo-raw. Maybe Mark was right and Grams only wanted to ensure she learned how to relax again.

No, that couldn't be it. There was at least one clue she was missing. Grams never did anything without a good reason, and she would see it through to the end. With renewed determination, she set her jaw. If it was the last thing she did she'd solve Grams' puzzle.

Mark took an exit off the business loop and turned left toward the Old Mill District shops. "I can't wait to eat. I'm starved too. Riding a bike all day has increased my appetite."

"I'd imagine so." Nicole studied Mark's profile. He gripped the steering wheel hard. Was he nervous about their date, or was it something else? Maybe Grams' game was driving him nuts too.

MARK WRACKED HIS BRAIN. How could he steer the conversation back to Sarah without giving anything away? Maybe he ought to get out of the detective business if he couldn't manipulate a simple conversation. It certainly wasn't the first time that thought had crossed his mind.

He parked. "I'll get your door." He strode around to the passenger side and opened the door with a flourish.

Nicole stepped out with a wide grin. "So chivalrous. Thanks."

He closed it and wrapped his hand around hers. "My mom insisted on raising me to be a gentleman." He shrugged. "What can I say? It stuck."

"For the most part," Nicole teased.

He opened the door to Anthony's and allowed her to enter ahead of him. They were seated immediately at a table overlooking the Deschutes River. Inner tubers floated by on the lazy current, enjoying the last couple of hours of sunshine for the day. He turned his attention back to Nicole. "How was your Fourth of July? Did you spend it with Sarah?"

Nicole looked up from the menu. "No. She was with Tina and Marge. I met them at the pool once. They are not my kind of people, so I spent the day reading."

He leaned toward her a little. "I'm sorry to hear that. I wish I'd been free, we could've barbecued. You must not care for Sarah's friends to spend the day alone. What don't you like about them?"

"Sarah says they're partiers. I'm not. Plus, they put off a vibe that bothers me. I can't explain it." Her face turned a rosy shade of pink, and she looked away.

The embarrassed look on her face intrigued him. "What are you thinking about?"

"Nothing." She raised the menu to cover her face.

"Oh it's something all right." He set his menu aside and gently pushed hers down. "Come on. You can't turn colors and not share."

The blush deepened, and he chuckled.

She shot him an annoyed look.

The waiter approached and took their orders then left them alone.

"So?" He raised a brow.

Nicole sighed. "Can't you let it go?"

"Nope."

"Fine, but remember—you forced this out of me. I was remembering a conversation I overheard between Sarah's friends, and it involves you." A saucy look covered her face.

His pulse thrummed in his ears. Maybe Nicole knew more than she'd let on. He cleared his throat and forced a casual grin. "The suspense is killing me. What did the trio have to say?"

"I think I'll let you wonder." She reached for her glass of water and took a sip, never losing eye contact with him.

Nicole could flirt with the best. But he had a job to do. "Seriously, I'd like to know." He heard the edge in his voice and winced.

She frowned. "What difference does it make?"

He needed to dial it back, but sensed she was about to tell him something. "I'd really like to know. It's important."

"Sorry." Her tone had shifted from flirtatious to annoyance. "I'd rather not talk about Sarah and her friends."

His stomach sank. He'd pushed too hard, and if the look on her face meant what he thought, he'd ruined their date as well.

CHAPTER NINETEEN

THE DAY AFTER HER DISASTROUS DATE with Mark, Nicole power-walked beside Sarah on the path near Fort Rock Park. A light breeze cooled her as day turned into evening. She replayed her date in her mind. Mark hadn't been himself from the start, but he'd struck a nerve when he wouldn't let go of his curiosity about Sarah and her friends.

That entire evening left her feeling uptight and like she couldn't trust Mark. Which was ridiculous since he hadn't done anything to make her not trust him.

"You're quiet today."

Sarah's voice startled Nicole from her thoughts.

"Sorry. I had dinner with Mark last night, and it didn't go like I'd expected."

"I suppose it's better to find out now than later, if he isn't the guy for you."

"Right." She honestly didn't know why she was so bothered. She knew things between them would end when he returned to Portland and she stayed here, but for some reason her heart hadn't caught up to her brain.

"Mark isn't the only bachelor in Sunriver. In fact, I spotted some men on the golf course this morning . . . *and* since you're sticking around I could introduce you to a few of my guy friends from church."

Nicole glanced at Sarah and noted she was completely serious. "No thanks. I'm good. I thought you were shy about those kinds of things."

"Not when it comes to my friends." Sarah slowed and stopped. "I'm finished for today. Same time tomorrow? Maybe we can warm up walking and then play tennis?"

"Sure. See you." Nicole marched to her car parked in the shade, and she startled when a figure moved from the other side and came toward her. She shielded her eyes with the palm of her hand. "Mark! I didn't see you in the shadows." Her heart tripped into double time as he stepped closer to her. This man had a dangerous effect on her.

"I was on my way to your place when I saw your car and thought I'd wait." He thrust the small bouquet of mixed flowers toward her. "Peace offering." He grinned sheepishly. "I feel bad for irritating you last night. Sometimes I get things in my head, and I can't let them go. I'm sorry."

"Forgiven, but really there's nothing to forgive. Thanks for the flowers. How long have you been waiting?"

"Not long. Do you have a minute to talk?"

She shrugged. "Sure. I was going to go home and change then head to the pool, but I'm not in a rush." She leaned against her car. "What's up?"

"I was hoping for a do-over dinner."

"I'd like that, but I'm curious why you were so intent to know what Sarah and her friends had said?"

He rubbed the back of his neck. "I can't say."

She narrowed her eyes. "Can't or won't."

"Can't."

"Oh." She wanted to question him further, but what was the point? Clearly something was up, and he wasn't going there. It was time to let it go and move on.

"I would tell you if I could."

A frown tugged at her lips. Was this a police matter? Could Sarah be in some kind of trouble? This train of thought had to be off base. No way would Sarah be involved in anything criminal, and yet he said he couldn't tell her, so it must be work related. She trusted Sarah and had a hard time believing the police would be interested in her, but she'd trusted Mark, too. Him not sharing why he wanted to know didn't set well, even if it was a police matter.

Indecision warred within.

"Nicole?" He stepped close and grasped her hand between his. "Please don't let this come between us. I've enjoyed the time we've spent together and . . ." He worked his jaw. "I need you to trust me."

"I'm trying, but secrets make it tough."

He nodded. "I understand." He stuffed his hands in his pockets. "Okay then. I'll let you go."

Nicole laid the flowers on the hood of her car and tugged him toward her. She wrapped her arms around his neck and spoke softly beside his ear. "When you can share what's going on, I'm all ears." She placed a soft kiss on his cheek and slid into her car before he could respond. Her face burned at her out-of-character boldness. What had come over her?

MARK WATCHED NICOLE DRIVE away, and regret the size of the Titanic filled him. His job had come between him and relationships before, but this was the first time he'd cared so much. One way or another, they would find whoever was burglarizing homes in Sunriver and soon.

In his gut, he didn't believe Sarah was a criminal, but he needed to protect Nicole no matter what. He slid behind the wheel of his car. A text came in from Spencer.

"Got something."

A few minutes later he walked into the station. Spencer stood in the conference room staring at the board they used to outline the crimes.

He knocked then walked in. "What do you have?"

Spencer spared him a glance. "Maybe nothing, but we got a tip."

"You think it's credible?"

He nodded. "A kid stopped by here a bit ago and said he overheard two people talking in the village. He took a picture of the women who were talking."

"And?" Spencer sure knew how to drag things out.

"He believes the women were discussing a break-in."

"As in planning one?" Could this be the lead they'd been waiting for?

"Yes."

"What has you concerned?"

"The logistics. Like I mentioned, he snapped a picture of the women, but I don't think these women are capable of carrying the stuff that's been stolen. As Nicole pointed out, many of those TVs are heavy and awkward."

"You can't tell how strong a woman is by looking at her, because women generally don't have bulky muscles. Can you pull up the photos? I'd like to see who we're dealing with."

Spencer handed him the prints.

Mark sucked in his breath. "Do you know who these women are?"

"Yes, and it doesn't bode well for Sarah, or Nicole for that matter."

"Will you give Nicole a break!" he snapped. "You know as well as I do that she had nothing to do with any of this."

"I didn't mean to suggest she did. I'm actually concerned for her safety. If she's hanging around these women, she's in danger. Whoever they are working with is trouble."

Mark nodded slowly. "Okay. What's the plan?"

Spencer laid out the plan in detail. "It will all go down tonight at seven."

"Why so early?"

"No choice. According to the kid, that's when they're hitting this house." He pointed to the map on the board.

"That's on Nicole's street! Again." He tightened his jaw. Why was this particular cul-de-sac so active?

"I'm aware."

"I need to warn Nicole."

"No way. We can't jeopardize this. I want that group stopped."

Mark crossed his arms. He couldn't let Nicole sit in harm's way, or worse yet become a victim again.

Spencer eyed him. "What's eating you? I'd think something like this would be second nature to a seasoned cop like you."

Mark glanced toward the open door and hoped no one heard Spencer. "Will you keep it down? I'm worried about Nicole." He rubbed his chin. "You have a solid plan, but we have to make sure no one gets hurt."

"That goes without saying."

Good, they were on the same page. He glanced at the clock on the wall before bolting from the room. They had one hour to set up. Not much time, but it would be enough. First, he needed to talk with Nicole and suggest she take a drive into Bend. He reached for his cell. It went to her voicemail. "Hey, Nicole. Umm . . ." What should he say? He hadn't counted on her not answering. Then again, she had mentioned going to the pool. Good—hopefully she'd stay there. "I need you to call me. It's urgent. And wherever you are, stay put. I can't say more. 'Bye."

Spencer breezed past. "Get a move on."

"I'm coming." He threw supplies into a duffle and hustled after Spencer. It would only be the two of them to start since time was short. He slipped into the passenger seat of an unmarked police vehicle and buckled in while Spencer spoke on the phone to the Deschutes County Sheriff's department.

Unease settled in his gut. He clenched his hand into a fist. *Lord, I don't like this.* What made this time different from last?

Nicole. This time he didn't know she was safe and out of harm's way.

Spencer pulled into the cul-de-sac and parked behind heavy brush so the car wasn't visible from the street. "Here's the plan. I want you in the woods behind the target house. I'll cover the front. A couple of deputies are enroute. They will wait nearby until I give the word to move in."

From his position behind the house, Mark had a view of the back entrance as well as the wooded island situated in the middle of the cul-de-sac where Spencer hid among tall shrubs and ponderosa pine trees. Keeping alert to his surroundings, Mark settled between large pines and a boulder. With any luck Nicole would be away until this was over. Satisfied he was concealed, he settled in for a long wait.

An engine slowed, and a van turned into the cul-de-sac and parked in the driveway of the house next to Nicole's. Adrenalin surged through his veins—this was it. He spoke into his radio and called in backup. He slunk to the side of the house for a better view but was careful to stay hidden.

A man the size of a professional football player stepped from the driver's side of a white, unmarked van. The passenger wasn't much smaller. They didn't appear to be armed, but a weapon was easy enough to conceal.

The men pulled two large boxes from the van and in no obvious hurry approached the front door, then went inside. Did they have the key? He waited, unwilling to spook them by moving in. Several minutes later the driver exited the house alone carrying the same box he'd gone in with. Where was that backup?

He looked over his shoulder toward the entrance into the cul-de-sac and spotted a sheriff's vehicle. Pulling his service weapon, he stepped out from behind a canopy of shrubs. A bicyclist bounced between the houses—Nicole! His heart slammed. She was riding her bicycle straight into danger. *Keep going like you don't see him Nicole.* If the perpetrators didn't feel threatened they'd more than likely ignore her.

The suspect glanced at Nicole and ignored her. Mark breathed a little easier and moved in a little closer. The suspect then looked toward the cul-de-sac entrance.

Spencer drew his weapon and trained it on the man. "Sunriver police. Don't move!"

Panic covered the man's face.

Nicole stopped and frantically looked from side-to-side, presumably for a safe place to escape.

Mark skirted toward her, staying low and using the shrubs as cover.

The suspect moved faster and yanked her from the bike, holding her in a headlock. "My friend and I don't want any trouble. You cops clear out of here, and no one gets hurt."

Mark's brain froze. Wild-eyed, Nicole whimpered and tugged at the man's arms.

"Let the woman go." Spencer edged into the street separating them.

He sneered and spat on the dirt.

Mark couldn't let this thug hurt Nicole. Nausea gripped his stomach as memories of Tracy's death flooded his mind. If only she'd answered her phone when he'd tried to warn her. He shrugged away the memory. This time had to be different, but why hadn't he tried harder to warn Nicole to stay away? If she got hurt, it'd be his fault—again!

His breathing slowed as peace washed over him. He took a deep breath and willed himself to stay calm and wait. So far he'd gone undetected, which they could use to their advantage.

"I can't let you leave with her." Spencer's voice was calm, but firm.

"Well we ain't leaving here without her."

Mark clenched his jaw. All things are possible with God, that's what the Bible said, and that's what he was counting on this very moment.

Inching forward slowly toward the giant of a man, Spencer chose a friendly tone. "The way I see it, you have a better chance of getting out of this alive by letting her go. You hurt her, and I'll hurt you."

"I'll claim police brutality, and then you'll be sorry."

"Not if you're dead."

Mark heard the steel in Spencer's voice and hoped the guy understood he meant business.

Their backup stood shielded by the Sheriff's SUV with guns pointed at Nicole's captor. Mark had a clean shot of the guy, but not if Nicole moved. It was too risky.

"The D.A. may cut you a deal if you cooperate. I can put a good word in for you—explain how cooperative you were."

The man's stance relaxed and his hold on Nicole appeared to loosen. "I'm no nark."

"Fine, but don't add assault and abduction to your charges. Let her go."

Indecision warred on the man's face. "How do I know, the second I let her go, you won't shoot me dead."

"I'm a man of my word. You let her go, you live. You don't . . ."

Mark crept up behind the giant holding Nicole.

"It's now or never." Spencer held the man's attention.

Mark took another step closer.

"Hold on. I'm thinking."

The other guy stepped outside. "What's taking so—" His eyes widened, and he dropped the box. The sound of glass shattering split the air.

The big guy released his hold on Nicole. Mark tased him. The man buckled to his knees. Spencer leapt forward, yanked the robber's arms behind his back, and slapped on handcuffs. Their backup moved in and arrested the other guy.

Nicole rushed to Mark.

"You okay?" He grasped her forearms and looked into her

shimmering eyes.

"I am now, thanks to you."

He tugged her close, and she trembled in his arms. "You're safe." He kissed the top of her head and ducked down to look into her eyes. "Hey, it's over." The adrenaline rush he'd had subsided, and his legs shook. "Let's go over to your place." He motioned to Spencer where he was headed and guided Nicole to her deck. She hadn't spoken again but allowed him to lead her into the nearest chair.

He pulled another seat across from her, and they sat knee to knee. "Talk to me, Nicole." Had she been traumatized beyond her ability to cope? He grasped her freezing hands and rubbed them. Clearly she was in shock.

Her eyes met his. "I'm okay." She spoke slowly as if coming out of a daze. Color crept back into her pale face.

"Yes, you're okay. I tried to warn you, but you didn't pick up." Like Tracy, but this time the outcome had been different. It finally clicked in his head that Tracy's death wasn't his fault. Sure he knew technically it wasn't his fault, but today he realized that no matter what he did, God was in control, not him. The guilt he'd been carrying finally subsided. He'd left Tracy a message warning her of the bomb, but she hadn't listened. He'd told Nicole to stay put but hadn't told her what was going down, and the result was the same. They'd both walked into danger. He couldn't control people or their actions. But praise the Lord, things ended much differently this time.

"I was riding and couldn't manage the bike and the phone, so let it go to voicemail. I pulled over and listened to your message. You could've told me not to go home!" The glazed look in her eyes shifted to anger. Her expression turned stormy. "You asked me to trust you. I did and then I was held at gunpoint."

Mark sat back letting her hands fall into her lap. She wasn't thinking clearly, or she never would have said that. "You're in shock."

"No. I'm angry. You could have warned me, but you didn't. All you said in your message was stay put—for all I knew you wanted to meet me there and save me a trip home. I had no idea I was riding into danger. You could have told me what was happening. I never would have come home."

He sighed.

The gate swung open, and Spencer stood there with her bike. "Where would you like this?"

"Park it there." She stood and looked down at him, her hands still shaking from what she'd been through. "I don't think I'll be free tomorrow. Thanks for not getting me killed." She walked past Spencer without even looking back.

The euphoria of a moment ago vanished. His gut wrenched. He hadn't thought about this from her point of view. Maybe he should have told her exactly what they suspected, but he did what he thought was best at the time, and he couldn't afford to second-guess himself. Hopefully Nicole would see that once she calmed down.

"Hey, man. Don't worry. She'll come around." Spencer clapped him on the back. "You ready to process the scene?"

Mark glanced inside the house and noted Nicole. "Yeah, I guess." He stood. "I messed up."

"No. We caught the thieves, and no one got hurt. It was a success, and everyone will be a lot safer with those guys behind bars. Don't beat yourself up. Give her time. She's in shock. I'll get her statement once we're done here."

He marched beside Spencer to the unmarked car sitting in Nicole's driveway. If he could do a rewind, he'd have told her everything regardless of the risk that she would inadvertently mention it to Sarah. Maybe he wasn't cut out to be a cop anymore.

CHAPTER TWENTY

NICOLE CLIMBED THE STAIRS TO THE loft and sat in the recliner. This had possibly been the longest day of her life. She rested her head back against the chair and ran through everything that had happened. It didn't take long to realize she owed Mark an apology. Sure he could have said don't go home, but she knew he hadn't purposefully allowed her to come into harm's way.

She'd give him a call a little later and invite him over, or better yet maybe she'd surprise him tomorrow morning and show up at his place with one of those giant donuts from the bakery. She would call now, but she'd heard one of the officers say it'd be a long night and didn't want to disturb him.

Needing something to do with the rest of the evening, she went to the bookshelf and looked over the titles. The spine of a Bible grabbed her attention. "That's it!" Why hadn't she thought of this sooner? She took what appeared to be her grandmother's personal Bible from the middle shelf. It had been there the whole time, yet she hadn't realized its significance until now. "Home is where the heart is." Grams had always said she felt at home in God's Word.

She cradled the Bible between her hands and sank into the chair. Taking a deep breath, she let it out slowly then opened the cover. Tucked inside she found a folded piece of paper. She opened it and read.

The game is nearly over. If you ever had any doubt, please know that I love you almost as much as I love my Lord and Savior. But He loves you more than I am capable.

Dear one, I urge you to return to your first love. Don't shut Him out a moment longer. I know it's been a rough couple of years, but Jesus loves you. He will always be there for you, even though I can't be.

You are more special to Him than you can fathom. Let Him comfort and guide you.

Matthew 6:25-34

XOXO,

Grams

Nicole blinked away tears. "Oh, Grams. I miss you." She gently folded the paper, turned to Matthew 6, and read. Grams was right as usual. God cared, and He would take care of her. She'd thought that when she came to Sunriver and started praying again, she'd moved beyond her old habits, but now she knew differently. She didn't need to stress about her job situation or anything else because He really was taking care of her.

He had provided this amazing summer vacation via Grams, and she had met Mark.

"Lord, I'm sorry for not trusting You completely and shutting You out of areas of my life. Please forgive me." Peace like she hadn't felt since she was a child washed over her. A smile tugged at her lips, and she knew that everything would be okay. She wasn't naïve enough to believe life would be perfect, but she would trust God with her future.

She leaned to the side, and the Bible wobbled. A business card fell out and floated to the floor. How odd. She reached for the card and noted Grams' handwriting on the back.

Call him.

Love, Grams

It seemed everything Grams had done had been for a reason. Well, whatever the reason, it would have to wait until tomorrow.

THE FOLLOWING MORNING MARK sat on his back deck with his feet up on the railing and sipped coffee while skimming the headlines on his phone. Though tempted to call in sick today, he wouldn't. Yesterday had been tough and the night had been long, but today had to be better.

The first thing he needed to do was stop by the grocery store and pick up another bouquet of flowers for Nicole. She couldn't stay mad at him forever, and flowers did the trick last time. Then again, she was pretty angry yesterday. Maybe he should stop in at the candy shop too and buy a box of chocolates.

"Knock. Knock."

His feet smacked the deck as he stood.

"Ungrateful woman seeking permission to enter her rescuer's lair."

He held back a chuckle. "Permission granted."

She pulled a bakery box from behind her and held it out. "I come with a peace offering." She raised the lid.

He stepped closer. "What have we here?" He peeked inside the box, and his mouth watered. "Maiden, you have pleased me greatly."

She grinned wide. "Good. I was hoping that giant donut would convince you to forgive and forget my poor attitude yesterday."

He grasped the chocolate glazed donut, took a bite, and then washed it down with the remainder of his coffee. "You made my day. And here I thought I needed to apologize to you. I'd planned flowers and chocolate."

She snapped her fingers. "My timing stinks!"

He chuckled and placed the pastry in the box. He stepped close to her and grasped her hands. "I'm so thankful you weren't hurt. I thought my heart would stop when you were grabbed."

She opened her mouth, and he placed a finger over her lips. "Shh." Cradling the side of her face gently with one hand, he lowered his head and brushed his lips against hers. "You are one surprise after another," he whispered.

Her eyes opened slowly. "Back at you." She cleared her throat. "So I take it we're good."

"Absolutely."

He glanced at his watch. "I hate to say it, but I have to get to work. Can we do dinner tonight? I'll cook."

"Sounds like a plan."

"Great. Six o'clock?"

"Perfect."

Mark accepted the file from Spencer and opened it. "What's this?"

"Read it. I think you'll find it interesting."

Mark sat in the nearest chair and skimmed the confession. "You finally got him to talk. Great! Do you think he's telling the truth?"

Spencer nodded. "He flipped on everyone for a reduced sentence. I guess he was a nark after all."

Mark handed the file back. "I'm relieved that Sarah had no knowledge of what her friends were doing. That would have been hard on Nicole."

"I agree. Those women were pretty sneaky. Offering to help out with the cleaning in the management office while they were visiting and saving everything onto a thumb drive was clever. I think the property management company learned a lesson too. Never leave passcodes laying around. Nothing like leaving the key to the computer right beside it."

"No kidding. It was definitely a crime of opportunity. I'm glad we caught them. How is Sarah doing? I imagine she was shocked to learn what was going on behind her back."

"That's putting it mildly. She's angry and in need of a good friend right now. I thought maybe you could clue in Nicole in case Sarah doesn't."

"Good idea." He pulled his phone out and dialed. Hers went straight to voicemail. He left a message then stuffed it back into his pocket. "If I didn't know for a fact that things were cleared up between us, I'd be worried that she didn't pick up."

Spencer chuckled. "Man, you've got it bad." He clapped him on the shoulder and walked away.

Mark couldn't deny the accusation because Spencer was right. What was he going to do? He'd be leaving for Portland before long, and she'd be here. He wasn't interested in a long distance relationship, but if things continued to progress between them, then that was what they'd have. *What do I do, Lord?*

CHAPTER TWENTY-ONE

MARK SAT AT HIS DESK WRITING reports. He'd be back in Portland by week's end, and the thought tore him apart. Nicole would be here, and he'd be over a hundred miles away. He'd miss her so much. Their relationship had grown so much this summer, especially in the weeks following the closed burglary case.

Someone cleared his throat causing Mark to look up from the computer monitor. "Hi, Sir."

"When you're finished with that report, I'd like to see you in my office." Captain Michaels strode down the hall out of sight.

That was odd. He quickly finished up and scooted from the desk. Several strides later, he knocked on the captain's door.

"Mark. Close the door and take a seat."

Mark did as ordered and waited.

"You've been an asset to this department all summer."

Ah, the goodbye speech. Wonder why he's doing it now?

"I'm sure you're aware that Winters is retiring at the end of the month, which puts me down an officer. I know it's not the big city detective job you're going back to, but we could use a man with your skills here. The job is yours if you'd like." He raised a hand. "Now before you answer, I know you'd be leaving a great position in Portland, but I hope you've found this place to your liking and want to stay on. Let me know your decision by Friday."

"Yes."

"Come again?" The shock on the captain's face was priceless.

"I accept the position. When do I start?"

A slow grin spread across his face. "Will two weeks give you enough time to settle things in Portland?"

"Yes, Sir." Mark's brain kicked into overdrive. He had a lot to do and needed to move fast to accomplish it all in two weeks, but it was doable.

Captain Michaels leaned back in his chair. "Good. Then that'll be all. Tie up any loose ends and take the rest of the week off. I want to see you back here September 13th."

Mark stood and couldn't stop the grin that covered his face. "Thank you." He went back to his desk and finished the rest of his paperwork.

Spencer walked past.

"Hey man. Hold up." Mark stood and walked with him to the exit. "It looks like you're stuck with me. Captain Michaels offered me Winters' spot."

Spencer slapped him on the back. "Congratulations! I guess that will make things easier for you and Nicole."

Nicole! He had to call her right now. "Thanks. I'll catch up with you later." He grabbed his duffel bag and headed out to the parking lot. Before he reached his pickup, he punched in her number, which went straight to voicemail.

"You've reached Nicole. Leave me a message."

"I have great news. I'm on my way over to your place. I hope you're there."

NICOLE PULLED OUT THE attorney's business card. "Here goes nothing." She pressed in the numbers and nibbled her bottom lip as the phone rang once, twice, three times.

"Miss Davis, I've been expecting your call for a couple of months. I see you finally finished the game."

"You know about Grams' game?" She shook her head. "Wait a second. How'd you know it was me, and why didn't your assistant answer the phone?"

"Caller I.D. I had the phone set for your number to go directly to my phone. I was beginning to think your grandmother overestimated your sleuthing skills, but I'm glad I was wrong." He chuckled then cleared his throat. "Against my advice, your grandmother orchestrated, with my help, an elaborate scavenger hunt that would ultimately lead you to me."

"Oh." So this was it. The game really was over. A mixture of sadness and excitement warred within her.

"I'm sure you're wondering about my involvement. Your grandmother was failing fast toward the end. She and I went back many years, and I was happy to help her. I was beginning to fear you wouldn't look in her Bible, and I'd have to contact you myself."

"It's been an eventful summer. I found the card a couple days ago but forgot to call you yesterday."

"I see. Ordinarily I'd like to do this kind of thing in person, but under the circumstances, we can talk over the phone. Before your grandmother's passing, she deeded all her worldly possessions to you, including the house you are currently staying in."

"Grams owns this place?"

"She did, and now you do. She's owned it for more than thirty years. It's been a great rental income for her. The home is paid in full and will provide you with nice revenue as well, should you decide to rent it out."

Nicole's stomach leaped. "Oh my. I can't believe it!" He went on about a bunch of legal stuff she needed to take care of.

"Thank you." Nicole hung up the phone in a daze. A knock sounded on the door, and she pulled it open.

Mark stepped inside and took her hand. "Are you okay? You're a little pale."

She looked up at him blinking back tears. "I finally finished the scavenger hunt. I can't believe this. This was Grams' house and now it's mine." She looked around her home with a new perspective, and it hit her. "This is where we stayed when we visited in the summers. I was young, not more than eight or nine, the last time we came, but now I kind of remember this place. It's been redecorated since then, and I guess that's why I didn't recognize it until her attorney jarred my memory." Her gaze slammed into his. "All my dreams have come true."

"I'm glad." He palmed her cheek.

A sudden thought struck her. "You know what this means?"

He shook his head.

"We get to go on some more tandem bike rides. At least until you head back to your job in Portland."

"About that. I've accepted a position with the Sunriver police department."

"For real?" The happiness reflected in her eyes had to match his.

"Yes, and I was wondering something." He pulled her close.

"What's that?"

"Would you be my girl?"

Her eyes danced as she nodded, and his lips found her. The game Grams had planned was more than a game—it had led her to her true heart's treasure—a renewed relationship with the Lord and a man she could respect and love the rest of her life.

~The End~

Books By Kimberly Rose Johnson

Sunriver Dreams
A Love to Treasure

Wildflower B&B Romance Series
Island Refuge
Island Dreams
Island Christmas
Island Hope

Standalone
A Valentine for Kayla

Series with Heartsong Presents
The Christmas Promise
A Romance Rekindled
A Holiday Proposal
A Match for Meghan

A Note from the Author

From the time I was first introduced to Sunriver, Oregon as a teenager to now, it's been one of my favorite places to visit. My youngest started walking at eight months old while we were on vacation there. It's a memory I will forever remember. I have a dream of one day living there, much like Nicole in *A Love to Treasure.*

I hope you enjoy the setting as much as I do.

I first began this story many years ago as part of a novella collection that never happened. I re-wrote this story many times until I was finally happy with the result. I hope you enjoy A Love to Treasure.

You can connect with me at www.kimberlyjohnson.com.

And Now—A Sneak Peek at Book Two
A Christmas Homecoming
By Kimberly Rose Johnson

CHAPTER ONE

BAILEY CALDERWOOD PULLED THE KNIT HAT her mother had given her last Christmas lower on her head as freezing wind whipped up her long hair, tossing it into her face. Wind whistled between the tall ponderosa pines that surrounded her employer's house not far from Sunriver, Oregon.

Not for the first time, she questioned her sanity in agreeing to move to Mona Belafonte's home. On a good day her employer was difficult to please, but now that she'd had a stroke, most of the time she was impossible. Not that she blamed the woman for being difficult. She had to be frustrated and angry at her situation and slow recovery.

Bailey needed to take care of her task quickly and get back to the house. Mona didn't like to be alone. Thankfully the youngest of the Belafonte brothers was returning from France next week in time for the holidays. From what she'd been told, he worked with the design side of the business as well as the construction side, and she was hoping having him here would brighten Mona's mood and speed her recovery. The task of freshening his cabin should go fast. But since it had been closed up for the past two-and-a-half-years, she expected there'd be a good deal of dust to contend with.

Crunching metal and shattering glass punctuated the early

afternoon air. *Oh no!* Bailey's stomach clenched, and her pulse jumped. The noise had come from the direction of the road. She jogged through the ankle deep snow along the driveway that wove through the woods to the road.

A small pickup with steam rising from under the crumpled hood had wrapped around a huge pine. The driver sat slumped behind the wheel. She bounded through the snow to cover the rest of the distance and yanked open the door. Blood streamed down a man's face. She fought rising panic. What if he was dead? She nudged the man's shoulder, noting his expensive suit and tie. "Sir, wake up." *Please be alive.*

"Don't." He pushed at her. "Leave . . . me . . . alone." His head rolled to the side.

She yanked her hand away. Was he drunk? She sniffed but didn't smell alcohol. What should she do? She'd left her cell phone at the house. He may not want her help, but he definitely needed it. She patted his face. "Hey, wake up. We need to get you out of here." No response. Maybe if she shook him—no. What if he had a head injury? She bit down on her bottom lip. A glance at the steaming hood caused her panic to rise.

She didn't think the car would catch fire, but she'd seen enough vehicle explosions on TV to prompt fear. He was too large for her to get him out on her own. She needed him conscious. *What do I do, Lord?* Looking around for anything that could help, her gaze rested on the snow. It was worth a try.

She balled clean snow in her hands and applied it to his head. The cold ought to wake him, and it would help with the nasty gash too.

A minute later, he groaned and slowly his lids opened. "What happened?"

Maybe he had a brain injury.

"You crashed. Other than the gash on your head, are you okay?" She wanted to shout at him to hurry and get out but forced herself to at least appear calm. No flames were coming from the hood—yet.

He shifted and winced. "I think so, but I hurt in places I didn't know existed."

If she weren't so scared, she'd laugh at his attempt at humor. She straightened and looked around to determine what caused the crash but didn't see anything—probably a deer or a patch of black ice. At least the engine had stopped smoking or steaming or whatever it'd been doing. "I imagine you're going to be sore for a few days. Your pickup is a mess and won't be going anywhere without a tow."

Her stomach swirled at the blood oozing from the gash on his forehead. She hated the sight of blood. This man needed her help, and she was the only able-bodied person around for miles. A tissue box on the floor at his feet caught her attention. "Hold on a second. We need to get you out of here, but first…" she slid her arm beneath his legs and grabbed a wad of tissues, then pressed them to his forehead. "We should stop this bleeding."

He jerked away. "Hey!"

"I'm sorry. I didn't mean to hurt you."

He laid his hand over hers. "It's okay. I've got it. Thanks," his voice gentled. He released his seatbelt and gingerly stepped out of the Ford Ranger 4x4. He swayed.

She slipped an arm around his waist. "Easy there. Don't want you falling or passing out." She chuckled nervously. "I've already got one invalid to take care of." She shot him a smile, hoping to ease the tension that hung between them.

He gave her a lopsided grin. "How is my mother doing?"

She released her hold on the man and looked at him more closely. He had the Belafonte blue eyes and broad shoulders. "You're Stephen?"

He nodded, then winced as pain shot across his face.

"You're early." She wasn't ready for him. Mona would not be pleased with her. "We weren't expecting you until next week." His crash had interrupted her mission to clean his cabin and make it homey. In his current state he probably wouldn't notice two-plus years' worth of dust, but just to be safe, she'd take him to the main house, then slip out and take care of the cabin once he was settled.

"Mother made it sound like she needed me, so I came back early. Are you her assistant?"

"Yes. I'm Bailey."

"Good to meet you. However, I wish I'd made it to the house first. Let me grab my bag."

Bailey watched as the man who towered over her five-foot-seven-inch frame, slowly ducked his head and reach across the seat.

He twisted back around, holding a small duffle bag. Pain etched on his face.

She pushed her glasses up higher onto her nose and stuffed her gloved hands into her jacket pockets. "Is that all you have?"

"I like to travel light."

"But you've been out of the country for a long time. How could you only have one small carryon?"

He quirked a grin. "Sorry, I was trying to be funny. The airline lost my luggage."

"Figures. You're really having a bad day."

"I've had worse." A haunted look darkened his eyes as he limped along the snow-covered driveway toward the house.

She adjusted her gait to match his slower pace. "I'm sure Mona will be thrilled that you came home early. Should I take you to the hospital, or would you like to come to the main house and let me bandage the cut on your head, and wait and see how you feel?"

"I'm fine. Let's go to the house. I'm anxious to see my mother."

STEPHEN GLANCED AT THE woman beside him, still trying to understand what his mother had been complaining about in her emails. Bailey seemed pleasant enough, even if the red and hot pink knit cap on her long, kinky hair looked homemade, and the too large jacket she wore over her jeans didn't do her any favors. It suddenly occurred to him that his teeth were chattering so he quickened his pace even though every step hurt. He should have thought to have his brother, John, leave an extra pair of boots in his pickup when he'd dropped it off at the airport. No one besides John knew he was coming home a week early. He'd been away long enough, and it sounded as though his mother needed him. He still couldn't believe she'd had a stroke.

He glanced toward Bailey and caught her watching him closely. Compassion lingered in her hazel eyes. She pushed her large, dark-rimmed glasses higher on her nose and shot him a look of concern—or was it unease? "Are you okay?"

"I was wondering the same thing about you." She rested a hand on his arm. "You're injured, just totaled your pickup, and I'm not sure, but you probably have a concussion. Who knows what else is wrong—and you're worried about *me*? At least let me carry your duffle bag."

He started to shake his head then thought better of it. What he needed was a hot shower, a painkiller, and an espresso. "Thanks for the offer, but I've got it. So tell me, how is my mother really doing?"

"I suppose she's doing as well as can be expected, but she's not a young woman, and from what I understand, her road to recovery will be long. She can't be alone for any length of time because she has anxiety attacks, which has made keeping the business running smoothly difficult. I can't do the job I'm being paid to do and take care of your mother. Sooner or later our clients are going to start complaining. I'm an interior designer, not a nurse, or a good cook or housekeeper." She pressed her lips together and looked away.

"What's wrong?"

"Nothing."

He stopped and gave her the look that had made most grown men squirm. "Even though I don't know you and my head is pounding, I can tell you're not telling me something. I insist you tell me."

"Fine, but for the record, dumping this all on you right now may be more than you want to hear."

"I'll take my chances," he said drily.

She crossed her arms. "I'm really worried about her. I take her to therapy sessions, and she doesn't seem to be improving. On top of that, she was diagnosed with type 2 diabetes, and she refuses to eat right. Granted, I'm not used to cooking for a diabetic, and I've been struggling with how to feed her, but she is such a picky eater. It's been a challenge."

"I hadn't heard about her diabetes."

"She's a private woman, so I'm not surprised. I doubt anyone besides her doctor and I know. Unfortunately, her mood has been less than happy, and she doesn't want to be told what she can and can't eat. I'm at a loss for how to help her." She snapped her mouth closed.

"I see." The diagnosis didn't surprise him since the disease ran in the family, but why hadn't Mom told his brothers? Surely one of them would have hired a cook for her. "I wish someone would have told me the extent of her problem. Had I realized how bad things were, I would have come home as soon as I learned of her stroke. I'm sorry you've been dealing with this on your own. I take it my family has been of little help?"

"They do the best they can."

What was going on here? It wasn't like his brothers to neglect family. Stephen's stomach knotted. If his mom was doing so poorly, why hadn't anyone told him, and why was an employee of their construction and design company taking care of her and not family? What had happened to everyone while he was away?

"Thank you for being honest. Now that I'm here, your responsibilities will shift to your actual job. My mom has always been a penny pincher and refused to hire out for work she can do herself. Considering the circumstances, though, maybe I can talk her into allowing me to hire a cook. But I make no promises. My mom is a stubborn woman."

She gave him a stiff nod. "Are you planning to stay in the main house?"

"No, but I will spend several hours each day there so you can slip out and deal with your actual job."

The look of worry in her eyes made him wonder, but right now he'd talked all he could. The house came into view, and he stopped to take it in and catch his breath. The snow set off the mountain-like lodge as if welcoming him home. "Wow, it still looks amazing."

She chuckled. "I'd have thought you'd be immune to its beauty."

"Never," he breathed softly and continued forward. Decorative greenery and pinecones hung from the cedar pillars that supported the wrap-around porch, giving it a festive feel. "Nice touch. Did you do that?" He motioned with his free hand toward the porch.

She nodded. "I started decorating last week. Mona plans to host Thanksgiving and Christmas here and wants everything to be perfect."

"I thought she was stuck in bed."

"Not anymore." She shrugged. "I guess she's improved, just not as much as I'd hoped. She gets around, but slowly and with the help of a walker. Some tasks are harder than others for her." Bailey led the way up the porch steps and pushed into the house. "There's a first aid kit in the kitchen. Take a seat, and I'll be right back." She scurried from the massive entryway and disappeared around the corner. He settled into the nearest chair. Nothing had changed in the two-and-a-half years he'd been gone. Not even the furniture had been moved, or the picture of him and his late wife Rebecca that rested on the mantel. He swallowed the lump in his throat and averted his eyes.

"Here we go." Bailey popped the top off the kit and tore the wrapper off an alcohol swab. "This will probably sting."

He sucked in a sharp breath when she touched it to his cut—she wasn't kidding. "How bad is it?" He studied her face for a hint at the condition of his wound. Her hazel eyes with speckles of gold gave nothing away.

"It's actually not nearly as bad as I expected, considering how much it bled." Her tender touch didn't surprise him. Bailey had an air of gentleness about her—she radiated quiet. No wonder Mother was going nuts. She liked constant action and noise. Rebecca and Mother had gotten on very well. She was like the daughter Mom never had. Those two together had been a force of nature. He chuckled.

"Something funny?" A beautiful smile lit Bailey's face. Her eyes sparkled in the dancing light from the picture windows.

"Being here brings back memories."

"Good ones I hope." She applied a couple of bandages to his forehead.

A whisper of pine scent wafted the air around her. She must have been working with the branches before she'd discovered his wreck.

"Mostly." He reached up and gently grasped her wrist, drawing her hand away from his head. "Thanks. I'll take it from here."

She stepped back, slipping from his grasp. "Okay. If you start to feel like you need to go to the hospital, let me know."

He started to tell her he could take care of himself, but the concern in her eyes stopped him. "Thank you."

"Will you be okay for a bit by yourself with your mom? There's something I need to do."

"Sure."

She still wore her outdoor clothes, and her tennis shoes were squeaking as she stepped past him toward the door.

"You should wear boots."

She turned to face him. "Excuse me?"

"Your shoes are soaked."

She looked down. "I'm fine." She spun around and bolted from the house.

Surely, she wasn't embarrassed by his comment. But something sent her fleeing.

"Bailey!"

He'd nearly forgotten about his mother. He rushed up the sweeping staircase as quickly as his sore muscles would allow and burst into his mother's bedroom.

She sat up in her bed. "Oh!" Mom's eyes filled with sudden tears that quickly streamed down her aging cheeks. "You're home." Her words came out slowly, but clearly.

He sidled up to her bed. "I am."

She wiped her eyes with a shaky hand. "You look awful. What happened?"

He could say the same about her but knew better than to comment about the side of her face that drooped slightly. Mom had always hidden her age well, but her seventy-three years were evident now. "I hit a patch of ice and wrapped my pickup around that old Ponderosa Pine I wanted you to let me take out years ago. That thing is a menace." He quirked a grin to make sure she knew he was teasing.

She wrapped his hand in hers and gave it a weak squeeze. "I'm glad you lived to tell me about it. Now, where's my addle-brained assistant? I don't know what's gotten into her lately. Ever since she moved into the house, she hasn't been herself." Her brow furrowed as she looked past him toward the door.

He'd only met Bailey a short time ago, but addle-brained didn't fit his impression of the woman. More than likely Mom's demands were frustrating the poor woman. "Perhaps you are expecting too much of one person, Mom." She'd always been a taskmaster. Dad had been a good balance to her Type A personality.

"Nonsense. I pay her well to do her job. She should rise to the occasion." She looked past him toward the doorway.

"Baily went outside to take care of something, but I'm all yours. What do you need?"

"A time machine."

"Come again?"

"I'd like to re-write history. No stroke for me and no accident for you."

He grinned. At least she hadn't lost her sense of humor.

"Since you are so quick to defend my assistant, what did you think of her?"

He shrugged, sensing an ulterior motive to the question and stiffened. "She's fine." He didn't see how his opinion mattered anyway. It's not like they'd be spending much, if any time together. He came home to take care of his mother.

"Mm-hmm, but what's your impression of her?"

Were they really going to have this conversation now? With a sigh, he sat on the edge of the bed. "I don't know. She came to my aid at my pickup and patched me up." He pointed to his forehead. "She's a bit reserved, but she's kind." He shrugged. "We only met a little bit ago." He remembered her gentle touch as she cleaned his wound and stiffened.

Mom harrumphed and crossed her arms. "Since you don't seem overly impressed by her, I want you to start searching for a new assistant for me immediately."

Alarm shot through him. This was not a good time to be hiring someone new with the holidays so close. Bailey seemed competent and was certain to know the ins and outs of the business. It would be difficult to train someone new. Granted he'd only just met Bailey, but his defenses rose for the young woman nonetheless. After all, she'd rescued him from his accident. Then again, if his mother wanted her gone, he should honor her wishes. He'd have to tread carefully with this situation.

Find this book on Amazon in ebook and print, releasing October 1, 2016.

42416770R00112

Made in the USA
San Bernardino, CA
02 December 2016